Advanced Healing Spells

Ember Academy for Young Witches, Volume 3

L.C. Mawson

Published by L.C. Mawson, 2020.

ADVANCED HEALING SPELLS

First edition. April 30, 2020.

Written by L.C. Mawson.

Also by L.C. Mawson

Aspects
Love/Hate
Justice/Loneliness
Empathy/Pain
Stability/Conflict
Loyalty/Betrayal
Trust/Doubt
Aspects: Books 1-3
Aspects: 4-6
Aspects: Books 1-6

Castaway Heart
Castaway Heart
Castaway Soul
Castaway Love
Castaway Heart: The Complete Story

Ember Academy for Young Witches
Advanced Healing Spells

Table of Contents

Thank you to all of my supporters on Patreon for helping me stress-buy Animal Crossing...

Special thanks go out to Seph De Busser and Peter Allan!

Cover by MoorBooks Design.

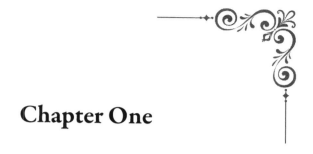

Chapter One

There are lots of things that I'd gotten disturbingly used to since finding out that I was a Witch.

First and foremost probably being the fact that I'm a Witch.

But spending my dream-time psychically linked to a woman who had been frozen for the last millennia, and who had almost killed me shortly after awakening was definitely up there.

But it's okay, we got past that.

Mostly.

Almost killing me had been an accident, and she was trying to help lift the curse she'd left on me.

And I was helping, given that there wasn't much else to do when I arrived at her tower at night.

"Wait, hang on, stop," I said as I realised what she was doing.

"What?" she said, huffing as she placed one hand on her hip, the other holding marigold flowers.

"You have to dry them first. You never use fresh marigold in a dermal solution."

Maria ground her teeth a little, but she did pull out her wand.

I shook my head. "How are you considered one of the greatest Witches of history and you're this bad at potion-making?"

"Because it takes too long," Maria admitted as she waited for her drying spell to work.

I grimaced. That would work, but not as well as letting them dry naturally.

"I take shortcuts because I don't have the patience for the long way, and then my potions are never that strong."

I took some more marigold flowers from her supplies and removed them from the preservation spell, putting them out to dry.

This potion wasn't going to be strong enough the way she was making it, so I might as well set up the next one now.

"At least you're aware of your pitfalls."

"Being one of the greatest Witches of history demands it. Especially if you're neurodivergent. You can't succeed if you don't understand your limits, Amelia. Pushing past them will only harm you in the long-run."

I folded my arms tight across my chest. "What if you don't like thinking about the fact that you're not good at something?"

She turned and gave me a reassuring smile. "Then that is understandable. But that's one of those pitfalls that you really do need to acknowledge."

I leaned back against the table I was standing next to. "Yeah, I guess..."

"For example, if you hadn't acknowledged that you struggle with Light magic enough to have difficulty casting healing spells, you would have kept pushing yourself to succeed in using traditional healing magic, rather than focusing on your connection to Nature."

"I don't *struggle* with Light magic."

Maria raised an eyebrow.

"I stopped you from freeing your coven by focusing on Light magic."

"I didn't say that you can't access it at all, I'm just saying that you seem to be favouring Dark magic. And why are you arguing? I thought you wanted to be a Dark Witch so that you could go to the Underworld and get your sister's protection."

"I just don't want to end up like you."

"I'm not a Dark Witch."

I frowned. "Wait, you're not?"

"No, I'm not Dark or Light. It's not a binary, Amelia. You can draw from both. Or the odd Witch like you can draw from Nature.

"I've never been a fan of thinking of it in the binary anyway. 'Dark' and 'Light' were just terms that Witches made up because the Demons and Council of Light demanded that we be one or the other to work with them."

"Why would they do that?"

"Well, the Demons didn't really. They started offering protections to the Witches who worked with them in exchange for making sure that said Witches followed certain guidelines and procedures. No one likes buying a healing potion only to find that it doesn't actually work, so the Demons created a sort of stamp of approval for the Witches they worked with. And then, since they knew that they could trust those Witches, they were allowed to enter the Underworld without much scrutiny, and they could also call on the services the Demons provided to their own people."

"But they let Light Witches have these protections too?"

"If they wanted them. But then the Council of Light felt threatened, seeing this as a Demon expansion onto Earth, so they created their own system. But they introduced the rule that their Witches can't have worked with the Demons in the past. So, every Witch was forced to choose. Unless, like me, they chose not to choose. But many did choose, and then it became easier if Witches working for the Council and Witches working for the Demons didn't mix across covens, and you eventually got Dark and Light Witches being split."

I frowned. "You didn't choose? I thought you were friends with one of the first Demon Princesses."

Maria looked away, her gaze darkening. "Helena wasn't exactly well-liked by her family. If you recall, her sister did execute her."

My stomach twisted as I remembered back to some off-handed comment Maria had made about her last girlfriend being executed by her sister.

I'd known that the two of them had been close, but I hadn't meant to step on a wound like that...

Maria folded her arms tight and the room warped.

Maria disappeared, along with the cauldron.

And in their place was a woman with long, ebony hair and murderous crimson eyes.

She moved faster than she should have been able to in her heavy onyx armour, her hand on my throat as her other held a sword to my gut.

"I swear, Manduorix, if you approach my sister again..."

"Your sister is a grown woman," I gasped, my actions no longer my own. "She can make her own choices."

"No, clearly she cannot. How can neither of you see it? You bring out the worst in her."

"You blame me for that? You're the one she could never live up to!"

"And coming to Earth was supposed to free her of that. She was supposed to find a new home here. She was supposed to find peace. And instead, she found you. Instead of letting go, she let you fuel her ambitions."

"I simply refused to let her believe she was worthless."

"And what about you? What has my sister done for you? I heard tales of a quiet Witch who wanted to use her power to help others. Now those tales tell a different story. A story of fear and of a Witch with no regard for anything but her own power."

"She wouldn't let people treat me as worthless either. Those people discarded me. All Helena did was help me see that grovelling at their feet wouldn't change that."

The Demon's gaze turned from rage to pity and her grip loosened.

Not enough for me to get free, but enough so that it no longer hurt.

"I'm sorry that I couldn't do better by my sister. And I'm sure that your clan would say the same of you. But this has to stop. I am not here to judge my sister, Manduorix, but the nobles are doing so in my stead. They fear that she is going too far, that she will create enemies that we will struggle to fight. We may not talk, but she is still a Princess. Her actions reflect upon the Underworld, and if she cannot be reined in, I will be forced into a more permanent solution.

"Please, Manduorix, I do not want to execute my own sister."

Tears welled in my eyes. "What would you have me do?"

"Break things off with her. Allow her to find the peace that she was sent here for. And find your own way. You both have the capacity to be great, but I fear that that greatness cannot be found together."

The tears finally fell down my cheeks. "I was going to ask her to marry me."

"I'm sorry."

The room warped once more, and I found myself back in the tower with Maria.

My hand went to my neck, rubbing the spot that the Demon had held me by.

"Something wrong?" Maria asked.

"What?"

"You looked dazed and now you're rubbing your neck."

"You mean that you didn't see that?"

"Didn't see what?"

I stared at her as I began to realise what had happened.

I hadn't moved.

It had all just been in my mind.

Or, rather, not my mind.

"Manduorix," I said, not sure how to articulate anything else.

Maria stared at me as if I'd grown another head. "How do you know that name? No one alive remembers that name. Even written records, my own books and journals as well as those of friends, no longer contain that name."

"No one remembers but you."

"Of course. I may forget many things over the years, Amelia, but not my given name. No matter how many more I have to choose."

I grimaced. "I think I saw one of your memories. You were thinking about Helena and then... And then her sister was holding me by the throat and demanding that I stop seeing her."

Maria frowned before turning back to the cauldron. "The connection between us is deepening. We have to find a way to break it."

"I thought you didn't mind that we can talk through the connection."

"Just talking is fine, but this...?"

"You would rather keep your secrets."

She spun on her heel to face me. "This isn't about secrets, Amelia. I have to live with these memories because I refuse to forget, lest I forget the lessons they taught me. But you should not be burdened with such things. You're still just a child, and there is still hope that you do not walk my path."

My heart ached for her and I moved forward to place a hand on her arm.

She frowned at my hand but didn't move away.

"What happened?" I asked. "I mean, I know that Helena was executed in the end..."

"I did exactly as her sister told me," Maria said, her voice barely more than a whisper. "And Helena... I may have put her on that path, but by that point, I was also her restraint. Her sister was right, we brought out the worst in each other, but after she'd already embraced that side of herself... Well, she did not react well to the break-up."

"I can imagine. I mean, I don't know how she felt, but you said that you wanted to marry her..."

Maria stiffened. "She told me how she felt in no uncertain terms when she left. That for all her sister's worry about schemes, she just wanted to have enough power that we would be left alone. So that no one would challenge the Princess for marrying a Witch over a Demon.

"And then when I was clearing through her things, I found notes. Spells she was working on so that we could have children together. Dreams of what our life could have been.

"I regretted my decision, but by the time I was sure that Helena's sister had made a mistake, it was too late. Without me, Helena turned her ambitions solely to the crown, and her sister ended up having to execute her anyway.

"There's not a day that goes by that I don't regret my decision."

"I'm sorry," I said, sure that the words weren't enough.

But I didn't have anything better.

Maria turned away from me with a shrug. "I have made many mistakes over my lifetime, Amelia. Sometimes I wonder if I've ever done anything right. I try, but I am constantly aware that it is never enough."

"You helped to save me from the Amazons."

She gave a cold smirk. "The Amazons only investigated you because I pulled you into trying to free my coven. Because I couldn't just be patient and figure out another way..."

She sighed, shaking her head. "After everything with Helena, I went home. I thought maybe her sister was right. Maybe my clan had regretted how they'd treated me."

"And did they?"

"I don't know. They acted like it, but then I saw how they treated the other Litcorde. Oh, they were nice enough to the ones without power, but the strong ones? They were under the same scrutiny I was. Subjected to the same fears that they might lose control.

"I left and started my own coven. I took the others with me, and we took in everyone who needed us. All of the misfits who needed a home.

"But as we grew, others began to see us as a threat. And that's when they beseeched the Angel to intervene on their behalf. And, well, you know the rest."

"That's why you're so desperate to free them? You feel responsible for them?"

"Of course, I do. They're my coven. I took them in because I thought I could keep them safe. I swore to them that I could, and then I failed."

"Do you have any leads on how to free them? If you need help..."

She gave me a weak smile. "Thank you, Amelia. But for now, our focus should be on breaking this connection between us. Or at least weakening it. I don't want to burden you with more of my memories."

"Well, we can give this potion a try once it's done. And if it doesn't work, I've put some marigold flowers out to dry."

Maria nodded, but she had that look she got when she'd already decided that she wasn't going to use it.

No, she already had another idea.

I suppressed a sigh. I'd learned to just wait until she sprung her new plans on me, rather than try to get her to articulate them while she was still formulating them.

"We should also focus on things at the school," Maria said in a clear attempt to change the subject rather than tell me that she had no intention of using the flowers. "When are you back in classes?"

"When I wake up. Hopefully I haven't missed too much... But the other girls who trained with the Amazons will be behind as well. It's why they're starting us back in classes tomorrow, rather than waiting until Monday. They want us to treat it as a day to get re-acclimatised with everything"

"And the Slayers?"

"They arrive on Monday."

"Are you worried?"

I shrugged. "Kind of. But as long as I keep my head down, I don't think they'll focus on me. Not like the Amazons did. They don't have the same motive to investigate a powerful Witch."

"I suppose not. Which means that, for the time being, you should be safe."

"I guess. Why do you sound confused by that?"

She shook her head. "I'm not confused by that per se, just... When I mentioned breaking the connection between us, I expected you to be happier about that option. My understanding was that the threat of the Amazons, and the fact that you needed my help with it, was the only reason why you didn't try to break the connection earlier."

"Well... I guess. But just because the Slayers aren't a threat doesn't mean that there won't be more threats in the future. And you understand Angelborn powers better than anyone, so I guess it just makes sense for me to learn from you so that I can protect myself in the future."

Maria hesitated for a moment before nodding. "Yes, I suppose that does, indeed, make sense."

I ARRIVED AT BREAKFAST the next morning with a smile.

"Someone's happy," my friend Lena said as I went to sit next to my girlfriend, Willow.

I shrugged. "I'm just happy to be back in regular classes again after everything that happened with the Amazons."

Lena rolled her eyes. "Nerd."

Charlotte shook her head. "No, I'm with Amelia on this one. I've missed my regular routine."

Lena gave her a sympathetic look. "I know. Have you got a sound-dampening charm with you?"

"I'll be able to handle the spell if I need it."

Lena gave her a look.

"What? I will. And if I can't, then you can say 'I told you so'. Speaking of which," Charlotte took a large bottle of water out from her bag, "you forgot to take this again this morning."

"Oh yeah, I'd been meaning to clean it."

"I know, so I did it last night, and I spelled it with dirt and germ resistance. I swear, every time you get sick, it's from this thing."

Lena took the bottle, if a little sheepishly. "Thanks."

Charlotte just shrugged.

"So," my friend, and roommate, Natalie said as she turned to me, "what was it you said you had first?"

"History," I said before biting my lip.

Willow leaned closer, placing her hand over mine. "You okay?"

I nodded, my heart fluttering and my cheeks heating at her concern. God, would she ever stop making me feel like this? "Yeah, fine. I'm just worried about how far behind I am in my Human classes after taking so much time away."

Lena shrugged. "Why do you still care about Human classes? You passed the Amazons' trials, Lia. You could just join the Amazons and never have to worry about interacting with Humans ever again."

I looked down at my avocado and egg baguette, picking at the edge of the bread as I tried to take comfort in Willow's lingering touch.

As much as I'd passed the trials, it wasn't safe for me to join the Amazons.

Not when their leader had it out for me.

"You don't have to be an Amazon to avoid the Human world," Charlotte said, probably picking up on my discomfort.

How she was the autistic one between her and Lena, I did not know.

"You could apply for Lorekeeper positions like I was going to. Lorekeepers aren't expected to have Human jobs, so you would mostly stay with your coven, doing magical research."

I sighed, remembering the warning one of the friendly Amazons – Esme – had given me.

That as long as Dana was in charge of the Amazons, I shouldn't go near them.

Which meant not joining any covens, as almost all of them answered to the Amazons, even if many did so unofficially.

My auntie was a hedge Witch, so I figured that I could be the same.

But after spending time here, where I didn't have to hide...

I wasn't sure that I was ready to go back.

"I'm sure I'll figure something out," I eventually settled for saying before picking up my sandwich and taking a bite so that no one could expect me to keep talking.

Natalie gave me one of her very slight smiles. An effect of her Vampire-side muting her emotions. "I understand that you probably want to stay away from the Amazons while Dana is in charge, but she might not be in charge much longer. Esme might win this leadership contest."

I frowned. "Is that actually looking likely?"

Natalie shrugged. "I don't know. It's an internal Amazon affair, so I've heard nothing."

Charlotte gave a hum of thought as she nibbled on her toast. "Well, I've taken up my place as an Amazon now, so why don't we go and see? I'm allowed to bring guests to Themiscyra, and I should go and check out the place they gave me at some point. Why don't we portal there tomorrow?"

I stared at her for a moment as I processed what she was saying.

I hadn't been allowed to leave the grounds since I'd gotten here.

Not outside of a short trip to the hospital when my mum had been awoken from the curse Maria had put her under.

But I hadn't been allowed at first because everyone worried that Maria was after me, and I knew that that wasn't the case now.

Then the Amazons wouldn't let me go, but they were gone.

And the Slayers didn't arrive until Monday.

"I'll have to ask my auntie to see if I'm finally allowed to leave campus, but if I can, I'd be up for it."

Lena frowned. "If you're finally allowed to leave campus, don't you have more important things to do? Like seeing your parents?"

I shrugged, glaring at my sandwich to avoid meeting anyone's gaze. "Well, if they want to see me, they haven't said anything about it. And if they do want something from me, I can see them on Sunday."

"Okay. Then I guess we're going to Themiscyra."

Chapter Two

Going back to my Human classes and finding out that I wasn't as behind as I thought should have brought me relief.

I was still on-track to go to any university I wanted.

It was the 'wanting' that was the problem.

I used to be so excited at the prospect of university. Of this magical place where I could go and be my own person.

Where I could start to chart a course for myself.

But then I came to Ember Academy, and it had become all of those things to me.

And the thought of going to a university full of Humans no longer held much appeal.

I hoped that things worked out with the Amazons' leadership election.

That they chose Esme, so that Themiscyra would be a safe place for me.

Thankfully, my Human lessons didn't drag on for too long, and I was swiftly heading to my lesson on controlling innate abilities.

I smiled as I entered the room to see Willow there, waiting for me.

"So," she said as I approached, "are you ready to finally return to Energy training?"

I nodded enthusiastically. "Definitely. I know the Amazons' training was supposed to be for the best of the best, but I don't think I learned half as much in their training as I do in one lesson with you."

A blush formed across Willow's freckled cheeks at my words. "Well, the Amazons aren't all they're cracked up to be. Now, where did we leave off last time...?"

Before either of us could remember, our teacher, Miss Tilly, approached.

"Amelia," she said, "congratulations on your success in the Amazons' trials. I was particularly interested to see you use an elemental healing technique." She turned to Willow. "Can I assume that she has you to thank for that?"

Willow nodded sheepishly.

Miss Tilly smiled. "More evidence that the Amazons were wrong not to admit you into the training." She then turned back to me. "But that technique you used... I've only ever seen it work for those with elemental powers."

I shrugged, not wanting to admit my connection to Freya. "Maybe I just have some odd connection way back in the family tree."

Tilly, thankfully, just nodded. "Well, if you need help with your powers, mine are also elemental, and I can likely teach you a few things. But that can wait. For now, I think you need to focus on your Energy training again. Willow barely started training with you before the Amazons came, and you could use the understanding of your powers."

I nodded, glad that Tilly didn't push when it came to how I might have elemental ties.

I didn't know whether or not I could trust the Faerie, and it seemed that almost everyone was figuring out my connection to Freya, whether I wanted them to or not.

And I didn't.

That knowledge was still dangerous.

Tilly then turned back to Willow. "Though, just to check, that is the extent to which you are planning to use *Fin'Hathan* techniques in this classroom, yes? I don't mind Energy training – other sects like the Wardens of Maltess have similar techniques – but I won't permit anything beyond that." Her gaze went to Willow's side, beneath her jacket, and mine followed.

There was the dagger her father had given her.

The *Fin'Hathan* blade.

"You never used to carry the blade," Tilly said, her voice soft.

Willow shrugged. "I'm not interested in denying my Elven half anymore."

"Your Elven heritage and the *Fin'Hathan* are not one and the same."

Willow just nodded, not saying anything.

Tilly sighed, presumably figuring that arguing wasn't the best course of action. "All right, I'll leave you two to your training."

Willow turned to me once she was gone. "Okay, well, I guess we should start with trying to channel Light and Dark Energy in turn and see how much you remember."

I nodded, though my thoughts were still on what Tilly had said. "Are people really so suspicious of *Fin'Hathan* techniques? I mean, it's just training, right?"

Willow shrugged, her gaze dropping. "It's not uncommon."

I shook my head. "It's ridiculous. Like how everyone freaked out when I went to Maria Brown for help. As if I was suddenly going to turn into her. As if you have to get rid of the good to recognise the bad. I mean, it's not as if you're actually going to join the *Fin'Hathan*."

Willow shook her head. "I just hate how Witches see fit to judge them. Especially when the Amazons answer to the Council of Light and they're as corrupt as they come. Say what you will about the *Fin'Hathan*, they wouldn't have allowed it to get so bad."

I frowned. "The Council of Light are corrupt? I mean, I don't think they should have sent Slayers here, but that's not necessarily corruption."

Willow sighed. "It gets into timeline stuff, but you know about the last Alternate Timeline, right?"

I nodded. I'd found some time for history books now that the Amazons were gone.

Especially after I managed to almost kill my sister's husband's husband because I didn't know that my sister had married the son of her enemy. Or that Demons could have two spouses...

"The Humans found out about magic, we ended up fighting them for decades, and the only way to fix it ended up being with a time-travel spell. But the spell only affects Earth, so magical beings who cross between worlds remember what happened, and some of them didn't come back to life, whereas Humans forgot and all of them came back."

Willow nodded. "The Council used to be democratically elected. Each faction would choose their own representative. But then they declared a state of emergency during the fighting, and we haven't had elections since. They keep saying that they're holding onto power because we need 'stability' in case there's another fight, or in case the Demons ever decide to try to attack us."

"They really think the Demons attacking is likely?"

Willow scoffed. "No one does. Queen Freya has been more than vocal in her opinion that magical communities should be more interconnected. But they claim that she's lying, and... Well, I say 'no one' thinks the Demons attacking is likely, but... A lot of people don't like them, and they're worried about how much power the Demons have compared to other factions. It's made Light beings afraid to tackle their own corruption for fear of it weakening them to an attack from the Demons. But the *Fin'Hathan* wouldn't have given them that choice."

"Yeah, as much as a sect of anti-corruption assassins does not sound like fun, after everything with the Amazons, I'm starting to see how someone thought it was a good idea."

Willow smiled. "My thoughts exactly. But come on, we should focus on your training."

ENERGY TRAINING HAD been... frustrating.

I hadn't wanted Maria to be right about me struggling to draw from Light Energy.

Even if she hadn't been a Dark Witch, and even if I had wanted to be one in the past...

Well, I just didn't want her to be right.

For her to know more about me than I did.

But drawing on Light Energy had been noticeably harder.

And the more frustrated I got with that fact, the harder it got.

"You're probably just still recovering from what happened with the Amazons," Willow had said as she took note of the issue, her soft touch the only thing keeping me calm enough to actually listen to her through my frustration. "This kind of up and down... It's more consistent with a Neutral Witch than anything else."

Even that didn't necessarily sit well with me.

If I was a Neutral Witch, then I was just like Maria.

So, either Maria was right about me, or I was just like her.

I didn't like either of those choices.

But then, the final choice was that all of the Dark Energy I'd drawn on was just some weird fluke and I was actually a Light Witch.

Which I didn't want either.

I was in a bit of a mood as I got to my next class, though it picked up as I remembered that I had Potions with my auntie.

"Good afternoon, girls," she said as we entered. "We're going to be brewing a healing potion again today."

Most of the class groaned.

Auntie Jess placed her hands on her hips. "Look, I know you can brew this potion now. But can you brew it with your eyes closed? Can you alter it as needed? Speaking of that last one..." She waved her wand over the blackboard, muttering under her breath as she revealed six scenarios written down. "Here are six instances where you might need to brew a healing potion. I want you to brew one that is as close to appropriate as possible. That means tailoring to age, species, and making sure that you don't waste materials by brewing more than you need."

She then counted around the room, assigning each of us a number.

I looked up at the board once she'd given me the number four.

A six-year-old has extensive burns. Her mother is a Witch and her father is a Vampire. Brew an appropriate course of treatment.

I went to my notebook and sketched up a basic healing potion before looking to my previous notes from the class to figure out how best to alter it.

Though I then flicked to my textbook. Surely a salve would be better for burns than a potion.

My auntie smiled as she approached. "Looks like you've got the right idea."

"I was about to ask. You did say 'potion', but the board says 'treatment.'"

She nodded before turning to the class. "The board says, 'appropriate course of treatment', and that does mean that if another concoction would be more appropriate than a potion, you should use that."

Several of the other girls tore up their current work.

Auntie Jess sighed. "I guess I'm still getting used to the teaching thing." She shrugged as she turned to me. "I wouldn't have held it against them, though."

"Well, it's sorted now," I said as I returned my attention to my textbook.

"If you want, I could teach you how to make the salve that I make for your scars. Not that I'm not happy to keep making it, but it's probably something you should know."

I nodded. "Yeah, I'd like that. Thanks."

"So, this is your first weekend without either Maria Brown or the Amazons after you. You know, assuming Maria Brown actually isn't after you anymore, but after she released the curse on your mum, I think I'm happy to take that chance. So, if you wanted to leave campus, you could. Maybe to see your parents..."

I shrugged. "Neither of them has contacted me to ask to see me."

"Because they don't know that you can leave now. But I know that your mum will definitely want you to visit."

"And Dad?"

Auntie Jess sighed. "I'm sure that he does as well, but..."

"But?"

"Things with your mum have been hard on him. He's not used to living alone."

I nodded, the news not really coming as a surprise.

Dad was always there for me, but hapless.

I guessed it made sense that when he had no one to help him out around the house, he also wouldn't have the time to be there for me anymore.

But the lack of surprise didn't mean that it didn't still sting.

Especially when Willow's assassin father still managed to make time for her.

"You don't have to worry about him," Auntie Jess said. "I've asked a friend to keep an eye on him."

"I thought Nightingale was keeping an eye on him."

"Well, when he needed protection, yes, but Nightingale's partner just got a job up north, and she was hoping that they could move in together now that your dad doesn't need such a watchful eye. But I trust Abigail to keep him right."

I just nodded as I kept my gaze on my textbook.

Auntie Jess sighed. "You weren't worried, were you?"

"Of course, I'm worried. Why wouldn't I be worried about a grown, able-bodied, neurotypical man having to live on his own? It's not as if I have my own things to worry about. Or as if I'm the child in this relationship."

Auntie Jess sighed at the venomous sarcasm in my voice. "Okay, that's fair. And nothing that I haven't said to him myself. But... I think this has all hit him kind of hard."

"And the Amazons almost killing me didn't hit me hard? Didn't warrant a single call or text?" I shook my head as Dark Energy crackled beneath my skin.

I'd been trying not to think about it, but now that I couldn't avoid it...

Now that I couldn't avoid it, all my frustration bubbled to the surface.

Auntie Jess reached over and placed a hand on my arm. "I know. He's being an asshole. And as much as it might not be my place to say, I don't think your mother's doing much better."

"At least she's trying. Even if she's entirely focused on taking me away from the school."

"Speaking of which, I'm sure that she will want to see you this weekend."

"So that she can try to take me away again?"

Auntie Jess gave me a sardonic smile. "Well, I'm pretty sure that she won't try to kidnap you if you go to see her."

I finally met her gaze to give her an unamused look.

"I was joking," she said. "Though... Just to be safe, how's your shifting?"

"It's still not funny."

Auntie Jess' smile widened. "You'll be fine. Though, in all seriousness, you should probably practice shifting anyway. With all the trouble you get into, you'll probably need a quick escape sooner or later. Are you free tonight after school? I could go over the basics with you."

"Okay."

"And can I tell your mum that you'll see her this weekend, or would you rather not?"

I sighed. "I'm going with Charlotte to Themiscyra tomorrow, but I'll meet with Mum on Sunday if she wants."

Auntie Jess frowned. "Themiscyra? Amy, I'm not so sure that's a good idea..."

"I won't be there long, and I'll be going with Charlotte and all of our friends. I'll keep out of trouble, I promise."

"See, you say that, but trouble always seems to find you, no matter what." She sighed. "But I guess Dana and her friends wouldn't risk anything in the middle of a leadership election. And it's probably best that you're not here while the Slayers arrive."

"I thought they weren't getting here until Monday."

"They start their investigation on Monday, but they'll be arriving over the weekend. But don't worry, they won't cause the same havoc that the Amazons did. They're just here to observe."

I nodded, but I wasn't so sure...

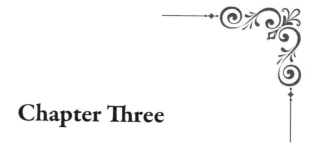

Chapter Three

I arrived at Maria's tower as usual that night.

"Here," she said, handing me the finished concoction that we had been working on the night before.

It was a thick, jelly-like substance and I took a little with my fingers and rubbed it into my scars, wincing as I did so.

I would have hoped that this mental projection of myself wouldn't be able to feel pain in the same way that I could.

But no, I might as well have been there in person.

Though, that also meant that if the salve was going to have an effect at all, it would affect my projected form, so I wasn't too annoyed.

Either making the concoctions at the school or trying to sneak them past the wards would risk people investigating me again if I was caught, and that was the last thing I wanted now that the Amazons had finally agreed to leave me alone.

But just as I suspected, the salve did nothing when I rubbed it into my skin.

Maria sighed. "Maybe it just needs more time to work."

"Maybe," I said, though I knew better than to hope by now.

"Well, I'm already working on the next batch, so hopefully that will work."

I nodded as I put down the tin.

Maria picked up a book before turning to me. "And you haven't had any more side-effects from our connection? No more of my memories?"

"No, nothing."

"Good, good. Hopefully, it won't be a common occurrence." She flicked through a few pages of the book before asking, "So, are you doing anything exciting this weekend, or just keeping your head down?"

I shrugged. "Well, I guess it's not really 'keeping my head down', but I don't think it'll be too risky. I'm going with Charlotte and the others to Themiscyra tomorrow. We want to get a better idea of how things are going with the leadership race between Esme and Dana."

"Ah, yes. I have to say, I am rather intrigued myself. I hope that Esme is right about having the support she needs to win this."

"Do you think she does?"

Maria sighed. "When I was living with Esme, she was liked by the Witches like her, but they made up such a small number of the Amazons. Most of those with power followed Dana's example, thinking that it was the only viable option. That they had to remain separated from Humans, and they had to focus on not 'losing' their power by having children with other species."

"So, you don't think she has the support?"

"That's the thing, most of those with *power* followed Dana's example. But as Mary Maltere, I was around students. Young Witches with no power, and who had, therefore, never been segregated from Humans or other magical beings. While the older Witches – those that have survived over the years, and through the War, which required power – follow Dana, the younger Witches stand with Esme. She's one of the oldest Witches alive, and yet she remembers ideas that were forgotten, not because they didn't work, but because the War crushed those who needed them.

"Dana and her friends thought that they had thoroughly crushed the old ways. That their ideas had won out because they were right, not because temporary circumstance had given them an edge. I don't think they're ready to fight against the idea of true equality and reducing their hierarchy."

I folded my arms. "I guess I don't know that much about their policy positions aside from the fact that Dana wanted me experimented on, and Esme didn't. And Esme also didn't stand for bigotry against my friends."

"Well, I know that Esme wants less segregation between the species, and she wants more cross-species projects to strengthen magical beings so that we don't have to worry about the problems with the Humans that's causing the fear that Dana is building her support on. What that would actually look like in a manifesto..." She waved her hand, but then stopped. "Okay, I could probably write it and have it be word-for-word accurate, but that sounds boring and I'm sure you'll get to read it when you get to Themiscyra."

I smiled at her words. "You really were close with her, huh?"

Maria shrugged. "I suppose she helped this new world seem less scary to me. I saw a lot of changes over the years when I was alive, but I saw them happen. Waking up here... It was a lot. And she made it less overwhelming for me. And showed me that there was hope in this new time. That the hegemony of the ideas that I spent my life resisting wasn't complete."

"So, now we just need her to win. You said the younger Witches supported Esme, how young?"

"Those under forty."

I frowned. "But Witches can live for centuries. Surely that means that Witches under forty are a tiny portion of the population."

"Well, as I said, a lot of Witches didn't survive the War, and the reason that the change happens at forty is because Witches older than that remember the War." She turned to me with a sigh. "If there is anything that I have learned over my long life, it's that trauma does not make a solid foundation for making practical decisions. I've fallen into that trap more times than I can count, and always regretted it."

She shook her head. "Though 'trauma' might be giving them too much credit. Like I said, the Witches who got out of the War got out with more power than they had before and working with other species would dilute that power."

I put my hands on my hips as I leaned back against the table behind me. "It sounds like, why ever people support Dana and whoever wins, it will be close."

Maria nodded. "Indeed. And if it's close, even if Esme wins, she won't have the backing to do as she pleases. Of course, the reverse will also be true of Dana if she wins, but Dana doesn't want to change things, so that would work in her favour."

"So, even if Esme wins, this won't be over?"

"No, I'm afraid not."

"Which means that I will never be safe with the Amazons, will I?"

Maria shrugged. "I don't think so. But do you really want to join them anyway? Even with Esme's changes, I don't think she's going to be able to change the elitist nature of the Amazons."

I sighed as I placed my hands on the table behind me, tapping gently against the wood. "I don't know. Not really. But what am I supposed to do after school? I don't know that I can go back to the Human world."

"You could always become a hermit like me."

"Yeah, but I actually like having friends."

"I like having friends," Maria protested, placing her hands on her hips before sighing. "But I take your point. Still, you could start your own secret island of Witches in the middle of nowhere. The Amazons don't own the concept. And then you could take your friends."

"I thought that was what the school was meant to be, but the Amazons act like they own it."

"That's because Gail rolled over and let them. I like Gail and I admire what she's trying to do, but she's so determined not to cause trouble, she's refusing to stand up for the right of the school to be truly independent. And that's what it will have to be to survive. Right now, it's a pawn in several different games of political chess, none of which will end well for the students.

"But then, standing up would mean conflict, and that conflict would put the students in danger. Gail chose the safest path for the students in the short-term, and while it might destroy the school in the long-term, I cannot begrudge her the choice.

"But another project wouldn't have to involve children. It could be for those old enough to make the decision to defend their home."

I stood up, placing my hands on my hips once more. "So, what? You're suggesting that I start my own Themiscyra, with blackjack and hookers?"

Maria frowned. "Well, you could have whatever you wanted. It would be your own island. Though, of course, I would argue for legalised sex work."

"You would?" I asked, deciding not to clarify that I had been making a Futurama reference.

Maria shrugged. "I've seen it come and go in legality in different places over centuries, but outlawing it always seems to hurt the most vulnerable, criminalising them for desperate circumstances. Or making it so that their only clients are those already willing to break the law. Regardless, as I said, if you and your friends set it up, you can run the island – or wherever you choose to set yourselves up – however you like."

I frowned. "That sounds like a lot of work."

"More work than trying to reform the Amazons from the inside?"

I groaned, having to give her that one.

She raised an eyebrow with an amused look. "What happened to the girl who said that she wanted to burn it all down?"

"She realised how much work that would be, and that it wouldn't be so necessary if Esme wins this leadership election."

"Perhaps, and I hope you're right, but remember that even if Esme wins, Dana and her friends won't just disappear. And the Amazons will still have to answer to the Council of Light, including the Slayers."

I ran my hand through my hair, knowing that she was right, but deciding to ignore that inconvenient fact for now.

I HEADED DOWN TO THE school gates that morning with Natalie.

The others were already waiting for us, along with Sarah.

Charlotte turned to me as I approached. "I asked Sarah to come along and help me settle in. I was too nervous to ask any of the other Amazons..."

Sarah shrugged. "I was heading back this weekend anyway. I feel like it's been forever since I've seen my husband and son."

At that, Sarah turned to the gates and opened a portal before stepping through.

I turned to the others, and they all had the same, hesitant looks.

But I steeled myself before turning to the portal. "Well, there's no use in waiting."

"I guess not," Charlotte agreed before stepping through.

The rest of us followed her, arriving in a stone corridor, the walls covered with portals.

"Come on," Sarah said, "we'll block the way if we linger."

We followed her through the winding corridor, which seemed to be spiralling outwards.

Eventually, we reached a set of large, wooden doors and we stepped through, into bright sunlight reflected off the white stone of the surrounding buildings, which weaved several paths down to the beaches below.

I got quite the view from this high up the island, but when I looked back, I saw that it went even higher, into a small mountain.

Just how far across did this island stretch? And how many Witches lived here?

Before I could spend any more time admiring the deep blue sea that seemed to stretch out forever before us, my gaze was drawn by a small boy, no older than ten, running up to Sarah before hugging her tight.

She grinned, returning the hug.

When the boy pulled away, he started to sign, and Sarah responded with her hands, leaving me completely oblivious to what they might be saying.

Which I guessed was fine. Their family moment wasn't mine to intrude upon.

Still, I figured that I should ask Charlotte to teach me some signs as well. I felt bad that Sarah had to rely on her captioning glasses when we spoke.

My gaze was drawn by another figure approaching, this one a tall man with bronze skin and violet eyes, decked in leather armour.

While the boy mostly took after Sarah, he did have violet eyes, so I assumed that the man was Sarah's husband.

An assumption that rang true when Sarah finally turned to him and signed what I assumed was a greeting before he strode forward and took her in his arms, kissing her in a way that made me look away.

Yep, they definitely hadn't seen each other in a while.

Sarah didn't seem as flustered by the kiss as I would have expected, however – if Willow had kissed me like that, I wouldn't have been able to focus on anything else – and she pulled away before turning to us.

"Chris, you do remember me mentioning that I was bringing some students with me, don't you?" Sarah both spoke and signed her words.

Her husband – Chris – gave her a sheepish look before also speaking and signing. "Ah, yes, I think I do remember you mentioning that now."

Charlotte looked him over, her gaze lingering on his armour. "You're a Master Slayer," she eventually said.

He nodded. "Indeed, I am."

I frowned. "What does that mean?"

Charlotte answered before Chris could. "It means that he's part of the ruling council that's in charge of the Slayers."

I turned to him. "So, does that mean that you know the Slayers' plans for the school?"

He sighed. "Yes, unfortunately."

Sarah turned to him with a frown.

"I just came from the meeting this afternoon. I was going to tell you once you got home, but if you think your students should also know..."

Sarah nodded. "They should." She then motioned to me. "This is Amelia. The student I told you about."

"Ah," he said, nodding before turning to me. "Well, I hope that you drag my wife into less trouble than your sister did."

I gave him a sheepish look. "I can try."

He sighed. "Well, I guess that's all I can ask. Come on." He turned to Sarah. "You said that you were going to show the students around? We can talk about work while we do so. And I think someone's getting restless."

He then nodded to the boy who had taken a dagger from his pocket and was playing with it.

I frowned before looking to see how many daggers his father was wearing.

Perhaps that was normal childhood training for Slayers.

Chris then led us through the streets and towards a market, where stalls sold everything from food to potion ingredients, with no need to hide the magical nature of the wares.

My throat tightened at the thought of being so free with my magic.

And at the fact that I could never be here as more than a visitor.

"You were asking about the Slayers' intentions for the school," Chris said as we moved through the light crowds, the chatter leaving me fairly certain we weren't being overheard. "Well, their intention is to take it for themselves."

I took a moment to process his words, the fact that he spoke them so plainly catching me off-guard.

"They don't like that Witches have a school and they don't," he continued. "So, their plan is to find any reason they can to make a case to the Council of Light that they should at least be in partial control of the school, and that it should train Slayers as well. And given that Maria Brown was successfully able to infiltrate the school, they don't have to find much else to have their case." He sighed. "I argued against it, but I was the only one."

I frowned. "But why go to all this trouble? I thought Gail's plan was to open up the school to other magical beings anyway."

"It is, but she plans to open the school to *all* magical beings. And the only condition Queen Freya put on her funding to the school was that Demons would not be excluded when the school was opened up to other species. There are a lot of Demons on Earth that don't have a home. If the local magical communities are dominated by Light beings, they're often excluded."

"Can't they go back to the Underworld?"

"Some can. Queen Freya has opened up the Underworld as much as she's able, but she can't take back those who were exiled as punishment, and many who were born on Earth don't want to leave. They just want a community here. The school was supposed to be a start, but the Slayers want to take that from them."

"Why does everyone hate Demons so much?"

"Because they're powerful. They're the most powerful magical beings. But their power doesn't extend beyond the Underworld. Not unless Queen Freya made efforts to expand her power to Earth, but she doesn't want to do that. Which leaves the Demons on Earth vulnerable."

Sarah nodded. "Freya was attacked by Demons a lot when she was younger. Lord Uther – the man who wanted her dead – would use the desperation of the Demons on Earth to get them to attack her. And then, after Freya had taken her place in the Underworld, Uther maneuvered her into a position where she had to exile some of her closest friends. Those friends can never return to the Underworld, and neither can their children. Freya never wanted her friends' children to become as desperate as the Demons who attacked her. Her first thought in funding the school was so that you would have a safe place to learn about magic, Amelia, but her second thought was of her friends."

"But if the Slayers get control of the school, they won't stand by the agreement, will they?"

Chris sighed. "They're hoping that taking control will create a loophole. That it won't be 'opening the school' to Slayers if they take over, and then they simply have no intention of opening the school further."

"Hopefully they won't find anything," I said, but I knew I didn't sound convincing.

Thankfully, no one called me out on that as we reached the end of the stalls and found one decorated with red and white ribbons.

Behind the stall were two young Witches, not much older than me, both wearing red t-shirts with white print reading "Vote Esme – We All Belong Here".

I grinned at the sight as I saw that the stall was covered in buttons and stickers, alongside printed pamphlets.

"Healer Sarah!" one of the girls squeaked before bowing slightly as we approached. "I'm so glad to see you. Do you like our stall?"

Sarah smiled. "I do. And I'm sure Esme would love it."

The girl grinned. "She came by this morning and we were so surprised! She even helped us set up." Her grin widened. "She was just so nice. And not like Dana. I interned for Dana a few years ago, and she was... polite, but you always knew that you were one of the unimportant people when she spoke to you, you know? Like she wasn't really listening. She never would have shown up before dawn to help us without someone having a camera out. Esme did it just because she was grateful and wanted to help us."

She then turned to me, Charlotte and the others. "Of course, it's not just that she's genuine. I'd vote for a smarmy asshole if they had her policies. If you're with Sarah, you're probably already voting for her, but here." She grabbed some pamphlets and handed them to us. "It's always good to be informed. And feel free to take badges and stickers as well. We want the support of younger Witches for Esme to be undeniable."

I smiled as I took a badge and pinned it to the blue shirt I was wearing tucked into black, high-waisted jeans.

"Good luck," I told them.

"We're going canvassing tonight if you want to come," she said. "We could always use more people."

I sighed. "I wish that I could, but I'm supposed to be back at the Academy tonight."

Technically, I was allowed to stay out, but the thought of being on the island for much longer was making my skin crawl.

The girls here were friends, but the rest of the island?

I was likely surrounded by enemies.

She smiled. "Ah, one of the students. I heard only one of you became an Amazon."

Charlotte raised a hand. "That would be me. The others are just here to help me settle in. But you probably don't want me canvassing. I'm Litcorde."

The girl shrugged. "We've got plenty of Litcorde on the team, and some of them canvass, but others help us to keep track of who we've already spoken to. But if you're a student, I know that you won't be here much and might not have time."

"Not a lot, but I might stop by later if I choose to stay the night."

The girl smiled. "Then I might see you later."

Charlotte nodded as we headed off.

"Good luck," I called back to the girls once more.

"Thanks," the talkative one said as we headed off.

Sarah then led us away from the market, down winding streets, as I started to feel a little more hopeful about Esme's chances.

Sarah led us all the way to the coast before stopping at the last house before the beach.

She turned to Charlotte. "This one's yours."

Charlotte grinned and I couldn't blame her. It was a beautiful little bungalow, with an amazing view of the sea.

Lena grinned. "Close to the water, huh? I approve."

Charlotte returned her smile. "That's why I chose it. I figured you would like the access to the water."

Lena raised an eyebrow. "Oh? See me visiting often enough that you chose your house based on what I like?"

Charlotte turned bright red at that. "I... Well, I didn't mind where the house was, so it might as well be here."

Sarah turned to her before Lena could say anything else. "Well, we should leave you girls to it. Charlotte, the house will recognise you and you can adjust the charm to have it also recognise your friends."

Charlotte smiled. "Thanks, Sarah."

"It was no problem. And if you choose to stay, that's fine, but I'll be heading back to the school at six if any of you want to come back with me."

Chris turned to Sarah. "I thought you were here all weekend."

"I am. I just need to go back to the school for a couple of hours tonight. But I'll be back. I promise."

Chris sighed, but he wore a smile. "Okay, okay. I guess it must be important to drag you away."

"It is." She turned back to us. "See you later, girls."

"See you later," I said, sure that I was going to be joining her at six.

That was as long as I could bear risking being on the island.

Sarah then headed off while Charlotte turned to the house. "Well, shall we see inside? And then maybe we can go for a swim. Not that I'm a strong swimmer, but I can watch."

I smiled. "Yeah, that sounds nice. This place really is great."

"I know. And maybe if Esme wins, you can come here too, and it will be a nice summer home."

"Don't count on it."

We turned to see two older Witches walking past us. They both looked around thirty, and one had a bag full of groceries from the market slung over her arm.

"Sorry," the one carrying the groceries said, "I didn't mean to be rude, but you young ones shouldn't get your hopes up for Esme winning. I know you're probably not old enough to understand, but she's just not a very good leader. She seems nice, but that's not enough. She's just not electable."

I frowned. "Surely the only thing that determines if she's electable is if people vote for her?"

"Well, yes, but they won't."

"Because she's not electable?"

"Exactly."

I did my best to maintain a polite smile, despite the fact that her circular logic was making my head hurt.

I thought the Amazons only took in the best of the best, so surely they were better than to vote on someone based on...

Well, I had no idea what this woman was talking about.

Dana had bad policies, Esme had good ones.

Why was there a question beyond that?

But then, I'd seen first-hand how flawed their selection process really was, so 'best of the best' probably wasn't accurate.

Or maybe it was a flawed premise to begin with.

But still, I couldn't fathom what this woman was thinking, or how she'd reached this conclusion.

But if she had, then how many others had as well?

"Well, sorry again for intruding. I guess we'll see you around."

At that, the two women left, and I turned to the others.

They were all wearing worried expressions that I suspected mirrored mine.

"Come on," Lena said. "Let's go look around the house."

I HEADED BACK TO THE portals at six along with Natalie and Willow.

Lena had chosen to stay behind with Charlotte to see about helping the volunteers with Esme's campaign.

We approached to see Sarah waiting outside the building, and she smiled as she saw us, holding up a bag.

"What's in there?" I asked as I got close.

"The final ingredients I need to wake up Aaron."

"Wait, really?"

"Yes, really. Now, come on. We shouldn't leave him waiting."

I nodded before eagerly hurrying after Sarah and through the portal.

"We should give you some privacy for waking up Aaron," Willow said once we were back through the portal. "Unless, of course, you want us to come with you."

I hesitated for a moment before shaking my head. "No, it's okay. I can do this alone."

Willow nodded before leaning forward and giving me a light peck on the cheek.

My heart squeezed at the gesture and I wanted nothing more than to take my words back and have her at my side.

But no, it would be hard enough for Aaron to wake up anyway, he should have my undivided attention when I apologised for everything that had happened.

For my part in cursing him.

I followed Sarah to the infirmary and waited patiently as she set up the spell, which involved placing various runes and lighting candles around the room in an odd, disjointed pattern.

It was strange, most spells liked symmetry, but this was a haphazard arrangement.

"You're trying to stabilise the spell," I said as I remembered the arrangement from Maria Brown's book. "The spell is keeping him trapped because he's the last component to it and it needs him to stay stable, so you're stabilising it without him before undoing it."

Sarah turned to me with a frown before sighing. "Of course, Maria was tutoring you, wasn't she?" She shook her head. "I should have probably asked you for help earlier. You might have helped come to this break-through earlier. But yes, I need to stabilise the spell first, and then I should be able to shut it down without risking any harm to Aaron.

"Do you want to help me with the spell? The more power we use to stabilise the spell, the less likely it is to want to cling to Aaron. And then I'll need that same power to undo it."

I nodded as Sarah finished her work and then picked up a notebook and handed it to me.

"There, it's that incantation."

She pointed to the words, but I frowned, unable to read them.

"Oh, sorry. Doctor's handwriting." She shrugged before taking a pen and rewriting the incantation in print. "I don't usually cast verbally, will you be fine to follow along anyway?"

I nodded. "Yeah, I don't like casting verbally, either."

"All right, then on the count of three, think of the incantation and that should tie us into the spell. Then we need to stabilise the missing strands." She indicated across the room, drawing lines in the air to where other candles would have needed to be placed to make the set-up balanced. "I'll place the remaining candles if you focus on powering the spell, okay?"

I nodded once more as I took my wand from my pocket and re-read the incantation over and over again, determined to get it right.

"One... two... three."

On the count of three, I thought the words and immediately dropped the notebook as the magic in the room hit me like I was a lightning rod, desperately searching for the missing parts it needed to stabilise.

Sarah moved over to the missing places, lighting a candle in each spot.

With each flame, I pushed back against the spell with my own magic, gripping my wand tight as I coaxed the spell to the flame.

As I did so, the flame shot up into the air, fuelled by my magic.

The spell's pull on me mellowed as it chased after the flame instead, settling into a more harmonious shape.

The more flames Sarah lit, the more it settled, until eventually, the spell left me entirely, happily flowing through the room without trying to draw on living hosts.

I gasped as the spell left me, gripping the edge of Mr Stiles' bed as a wave of exhaustion almost knocked me off my feet.

"Hold on, Amelia," Sarah said as she made her way back over to me. "This spell won't let him go completely until we undo it."

"And how do we do that?"

"If we extinguish the flames all at once, it should shut the spell down too quickly, robbing it of the power it needs to find a new host to draw on."

"Right. I can do that."

I didn't have to think about it much, the exhaustion shutting down my ability to think straight and letting something else, something more primal, in.

I snapped my wand-less hand into a fist and a gust of air shot through the room, extinguishing every flame at once.

Sarah turned back to me. "Did you use a spell there?"

I nodded. "Yeah. I couldn't tell you the incantation, but... I did manipulate the surrounding magic in the air to get it to act like that. Why?"

"You didn't use your wand. It looked more like how Freya uses her Elemental powers."

I shrugged. "I do still have my wand in my hand. I think just moving my other hand helped me focus."

Sarah examined me for a moment before Mr Stiles groaned from his bed, drawing my attention, and then Sarah's.

"Aaron," Sarah said as he attempted to push himself up. "Be careful."

She moved over to help him sit up.

He groaned, squinting as if even the low light of the evening was hurting his eyes. "Sarah? When did you get here? How long was I out for? I feel like shit."

He clumsily attempted to sign as he spoke, but it was clear that he was struggling to move his hands, just as he was struggling to speak, his voice raspy and strained.

"Here," Sarah said, passing him a purple tea. "You need to get your strength back."

He nodded before taking the tea and downing it in nearly one go.

He still looked uncomfortable with the light, so I flicked my wand, drawing the blinds closed.

"Thanks," he said with a smile as he turned to me. "Well, Amelia, you're still alive and well, and we're still at the school, so your news can't be that bad, Sarah."

Sarah fixed him with an annoyed look. "You were out for weeks."

He raised his eyebrows. "Huh... I'm guessing Maria had me under quite the nasty curse if it's taken you this long to lift it."

My throat tightened at the reminder of my part in all of it. "I'm sorry," I said. "It's my fault that she was able to curse you. I just..."

"It's okay," Mr Stiles said with a sigh. "From Maria's taunting in the maze, I can guess at what happened. You could see through my glamour, and the fact that I was hiding who I was made you suspicious. Especially given that Maria first sent Demons after you, not Witches. And my warnings about Maria probably looked like an enemy trying to warn you away from a friend, not the other way around." He ran a hand through his long hair with a sigh. "I shouldn't have lied to you about who I was. Not after you broke through. Freya didn't want you to feel pressured to be a Dark Witch because she was looking out for you, but I was the one on the ground and I knew that the situation had changed."

He gave a hollow laugh. "When did I become the kind of Demon who got in trouble for *following* orders?"

Sarah smiled. "You're getting old."

He groaned. "Don't remind me." He turned back to me. "And it really is okay, Amelia. Apology accepted. You made a bad call, it happens. The key is to learn from it going forward, okay?"

I nodded, not sure what else to say.

Mr Stiles smiled before turning back to Sarah. "So, how big of a shit-show was it after I was cursed?"

"The Amazons came to investigate and tried to get Amelia under their control once they realised how powerful she was."

"Of course, they did. Did they ever figure out where her power came from? And her connection to Freya?"

"No, nothing like that. The Amazons tried to claim that Amelia was too powerful and lacked training as a justification for taking her to Themiscyra, but she passed their trials. Though it was a close thing and Esme had to challenge Dana to save her."

Mr Stiles sighed. "Which means the Amazons are having an election. That was a risky move. Well, I hope Esme's sure of her support."

"It's going to be close, no matter which way it goes. And Dana also went to the Council of Light and reported on the situation here. Whatever Dana said, it was enough for the Council to launch an investigation of their own. Luckily, Amelia seems to be off their radar, but they've sent Slayers to evaluate the school."

Mr Stiles frowned. "If Slayers are coming, you might have been better off leaving me unconscious. They won't like my presence here, and a suffering Demon might have put them in a better mood."

Sarah didn't seem amused by his joke. "You were under a spell cast by Maria Brown. Leaving you under it for any longer than necessary would have been too risky."

"You just didn't want to explain it to Damon if I died. He's got too much puppy-dog energy for anyone to ever want to hurt him."

Sarah sighed. "Or I'm a doctor and I care about my patients living."

"Well, that too."

Sarah shook her head. "Speaking of being under Maria Brown's spell for so long, how do you feel? The restorative potion should have helped a little, but..."

"I feel fine," he assured her, and Sarah frowned as she looked him over.

He did, indeed, seem fine. Rather startlingly fine, given how awful he'd looked just moments ago.

"Huh," Sarah said. "I guess I did a better job than I thought." She turned to me. "Though that is probably down to your help, so thank you, Amelia."

I nodded, just glad that I could help put this right.

The door to the infirmary then opened, drawing our attention.

Gail strode through, though her steps slowed as she saw Mr Stiles awake, and she gave him a relieved smile. "Aaron, thank the Creator. When Sarah said that she thought she had what she needed to bring you back, I couldn't have been more relieved. I'm so sorry, I should have realised that Mary was Maria earlier."

Mr Stiles shook his head. "Okay, everyone needs to stop apologising to me. This was my fault as much as anyone else's. I should be the one apologising to you, Gail, for not telling you who Mary was as soon as I figured it out, rather than going off to deal with the problem myself."

"And for not telling me that Queen Freya sent you here to the school to protect Amelia."

"Well, yes, that as well, but I had orders."

"And Queen Freya knows me. Why wouldn't she trust me with this?"

Mr Stiles gave her an apologetic look. "I'm afraid that Freya doesn't trust anyone with information regarding her connection to Amelia. If Amelia wants to come to the Underworld when she's older, she'll be welcomed with open arms, but the danger of being the Queen's sister shouldn't be forced on her now."

"Except she's already in danger. She's more powerful than she should be, did Queen Freya really think that would stay hidden?"

Mr Stiles sighed. "In all honesty, we have no idea how that happened. Freya knew that she would be powerful, but this powerful?"

Sarah spoke up at that. "Actually, we do know now. Maria Brown is powerful in the same way and told Amelia that she's 'Angelborn'. It looks like Freya gave her part of her power by accident."

Gail shook her head. "Which is something I could have told you about if you had included me in this. But instead, I've been cleaning up behind everyone and now the school is under suspicion."

Mr Stiles gave her an apologetic look. "You're right, I'm sorry."

Gail folded her arms. "It's okay. It was a difficult situation and focusing on what we could have done better in the past won't help us now."

Mr Stiles nodded. "Well, in the future, I promise to be completely honest with you. Assuming that I'm still welcome here and my job is still available."

Gail gave him a small smile. "You think I've had time to find a replacement with everything else going on? No, another member of staff would be very much appreciated right now. Though the Slayers might not be happy about a Demon teaching here..."

"If you would prefer that I don't return to my job..."

Gail frowned in thought for a moment before shaking her head. "No. They cannot build a case against the school based on your presence alone – assuming that your teaching credentials weren't entirely fabricated – and you might actually serve as something to distract their attention from other issues that might make a stronger case."

"Are there many such issues?"

Gail sighed. "It's a brand-new school, Aaron. I'm sure that they could find something if they looked hard enough. But with you drawing their eye, they might not look hard enough. Assuming that you are up for being scrutinised in such a way."

Aaron nodded with a smile. "I grew up a gay, noble Demon before heartbonds were brought back into fashion, Gail. I can withstand scrutiny. And as for my teaching credentials, I'm in charge of teaching the new Queensguard recruits pretty much everything except fighting. Damon handles that. But spellcasting, rune-making, potion brewing and healing? That's all me."

"I didn't realise Queen Freya's guard needed such skills."

Aaron smiled. "It's not all sword-fights to protect the Queen."

"Well then, I guess it's good to have you back, Mr Stiles."

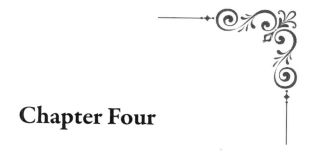

Chapter Four

"Sarah got Mr Stiles awake again," I said almost as soon as I arrived in Maria's tower.

Maria frowned. "She did? You're sure?"

I folded my arms, watching her warily. "Why are you asking as if it's a bad thing? I thought you regretted cursing him."

"I do! I just... I'm just surprised. I thought unravelling that spell would take years. But I suppose I underestimated Sarah. And if Aaron's awake again, then all of the focus I was dedicating to helping him can now be entirely focused on helping you."

"On breaking our connection, you mean?"

"Well, yes, but isn't that what you want? You must be tired of coming here every night. And as I said, I don't want to inflict any more of my memories on you."

I nodded, though I wasn't sure how I felt about it.

I realised that if the connection was broken, I would miss coming here at night.

After everything with the Amazons, it almost felt like a refuge.

One last place I could go for help if everywhere else failed me.

"If you break the connection, is there any way that we could still talk? I mean, no one knows about the connection aside from my friends, so there's no risk in us talking like this, but if we break it..."

Maria sighed. "If we break it, there will be a chance that any other form of communication will be found and then either traced back to me or used to implicate you as a co-conspirator of mine." She snorted at

45

the idea before shaking her head. "No, there's no safe way for now. Not while you're at the school. But once you're finished your education, feel free to come and join me out here."

I let out a snort of my own. "It might be the only magical place that will take me..."

"Unless you start somewhere of your own."

"Yes, I suppose." I looked around the room. "Are you really not lonely up here? I mean, why don't you start an island to rival the Amazons?"

"I might, but not now. Not until I free my coven."

There was an icy determination in her voice, and I stumbled a little as the world warped around me, just as it had the last time I'd been in Maria's memories.

I was still in the tower, but it was no longer so quiet.

Three other Witches were with me, one a young girl, and the other two young women, one of whom had a toddler on her hip.

"You're sure it's an ear infection?" the woman with the toddler asked. "She's drawing blood..."

"She's trying to get the pain out," I told the woman as I made my way across the room to the cauldron that the other young woman was tending to. "Isn't that right, Alix?"

The teenager nodded before turning to the woman with the baby and signing with her hands.

The woman sighed. "Okay, okay. I just... Emma neither signs nor talks yet, and she keeps hurting herself. I'm Litcorde and I never hurt myself."

I turned to her with a frown. "Giselle, you are constantly pulling your eyebrows out or scratching the insides of your arms."

"Yes, okay, but they're not real hurts. I don't draw blood."

"And Emma is still very young. And probably in a lot of pain right now." I sighed as I made my way over to Giselle and placed a hand on her shoulder. "I've been working on a charm that can make pictures from thoughts. Maybe she'll like that as a communication tool."

"Maybe..."

"And if she doesn't, we have other tools to try. No one gets left behind here, Giselle. Not you and not Emma. And if you need a babysitter for a while, just ask. When was the last time you got a full night's sleep?"

"It... It's been a while."

"Why don't you leave Emma with me for the night? I'll administer the healing potion and see about getting her to use this charm."

Giselle smiled as she handed me the toddler. "Thank you, Maria. I have no idea what I would do without you."

The tower dissolved back into its current form and I caught Maria watching me carefully.

"Another memory?" she asked.

I nodded. "You really cared for your coven, didn't you?"

"Of course, I did."

"It... It seemed like you were a good Coven Head."

Maria snorted. "That's what I would have said, too. Before the Angel came and decided to curse us all for my mistakes..."

I moved over to her and placed a hand on her arm. "I promise, we'll figure out how to get them free. And I'll help, however I can."

Maria gave me a bittersweet smile. "Thank you, Amelia. That really does mean a lot."

She then moved away, across to the many tomes on her shelf and started browsing, as she so often did when we started talking about things that made her uncomfortable.

Mostly her past.

"So," Maria said as she finally picked up a book on healing, "how did your trip to Themiscyra go?"

"Fine. Charlotte settled in fine."

"And did you hear anything about Esme's campaign?"

"Nothing that we didn't already know," I said with a sigh. "The younger Witches were enthusiastically supportive, but the older ones were really dismissive of her. They said that she wasn't 'electable'."

"What does that mean?"

"I have no idea."

Maria shook her head. "Sounds like a coded way to say that they agree with Dana's policies but don't want to say that out loud because they know it would sound awful to actually voice the policies aloud."

"Like that the number of mixed-species Amazon recruits has dropped drastically since Dana took charge?" I said, quoting from the pamphlet the girls at Esme's stall had given me. I hadn't had the chance to check the statistic myself, given that it wouldn't be easily available online, but Charlotte had promised to double-check the facts in the pamphlet.

She'd texted that night, saying that the Amazon Lorekeepers had helped find the statistics and were more than happy to verify every single one of them.

When Charlotte had asked if they could do the same for anything Dana was apparently saying, they hadn't been able to.

Maria nodded. "Exactly. I may be being uncharitable, maybe there really is some aspect that Litcorde and Sisters are oblivious to, but with the future of Witches at stake, I'm not feeling charitable." She shook her head. "No, saying that the future of Witches is at stake is thinking too narrowly. Like I said, you can always start your own Amazons."

I sighed. "Yeah, I just hope it doesn't come to that."

"So, I take it you aren't going to risk going back tomorrow?"

"No, definitely not. Actually, I'm going to see my mum."

Maria raised an eyebrow. "Oh? How do you see that going?"

I folded my arms. "I have no idea."

"And your father? Has he been in contact with you?"

I sighed. "No, he hasn't."

She gave me an understanding look and nodded. "Well, however it goes, remember that you've got other people that care about you."

I nodded, knowing that she was right, but that didn't make the prospect of facing the next morning any easier.

I ARRIVED AT MY AUNTIE's house the next morning and knocked on the door before opening it.

I was going to call to her to let her know that I'd arrived, but then I heard voices from the kitchen.

"Have you spoken to Damon yet?"

I quietly moved to the door to see that Auntie Jess was talking to Mr Stiles.

Mr Stiles smiled. "Yeah, I called him last night. He must have been really worried for me, I'm sure that it was taking all of his willpower to not either show up here or order me home."

"You say that as if you ever follow his orders."

Mr Stiles shrugged. "Well, if I obeyed every order, Damon never would have been comfortable with our relationship.

"But as much as he wanted to see me – and as much as I miss him – we both agreed that I'm better off staying here right now. The Slayers might not be looking to examine Amelia all that carefully, but she could still use as much protection as we can give."

He sighed, running his hand through his hair. "Freya's worried about what happened with Maria Brown. About how close Maria got to Amelia, even though we were all on high alert. I'm determined to make sure that her worries never mean anything."

"Me too," Auntie Jess said. "Though when it comes to the Slayers, my worry is less that they'll do something to Amy directly, but that they'll get the school shut down out of spite and she'll have nowhere else to go. I like being a hedge Witch, but I recognise that it isn't suited to everyone. Amy should have more time around other Witches, but if the school closes, I don't know where else she could safely get that."

"What does Gail think about the threat the Slayers pose?"

"She's terrified. I'm trying to help as best I can, but... She needs someone she can rely on, and I've never been that."

Mr Stiles sighed. "I would argue with that, but I get the feeling that I would be stepping on old history."

"Old history that is too far gone to repair, I fear. Regardless, Gail is right to worry about the threat that the Slayers pose to the school. If they can make the case that Gail hasn't been adequately protecting the students..."

"Such a case would require evidence, and Gail is too good at her job for there to be much against her. And what is there can be put down to this being an ambitious project that is only in its second year. No one could have expected better from her."

"That assumes that the Council of Light has reasonable expectations."

"Perhaps. But even if they don't, Esme may still become the leader of the Amazons, and I don't think the Council will fight the Amazons over the school."

Auntie Jess sighed, shaking her head. "Except Esme isn't going to win the leadership contest, Aaron. She's nice, but she's not electable. No one's going to vote for her."

My stomach twisted with worry at that assessment.

I had no idea what my auntie thought wasn't electable about Esme, but she'd been part of this magical world longer than me.

What if she was right?

What if there was something I was missing, and Esme wouldn't get elected?

Then I would be barred from the magical world as soon as I leave school.

All except for the Underworld.

Or, as Maria suggested, starting my own version of the Amazons.

Maybe that wasn't the worst idea after all...

I suppressed a sigh. I really didn't want a mission, I just wanted to finish school.

I hoped that the Amazons would give me a choice in that.

Aaron shook his head. "You forget that I was raised a noble. I know politics well, Jess. That sounds like something that Dana and her friends keep repeating until it sticks, not something that's actually true."

"But if it sticks, what does that matter?"

I decided to knock on the door at that point, not sure my nerves can take much more of this speculation.

My auntie turned to me with a smile. "Amy. Good morning. How was your trip yesterday?"

I shrugged. "It was fine. Charlotte's new place seemed nice."

"And you managed to stay out of trouble?"

"Yes, I promise."

Aaron chuckled at that before turning to me. "It's good to see you again, Amelia. We didn't get much of a chance to talk last night with everyone else swarming in. How are you? How have your studies been going?"

I shrugged. "I'm doing fine. Especially now that the Amazons aren't threatening to experiment on me. And my studies have been going fine as well. I'm actually pretty good with elemental magic, so my friends are helping me learn."

He nodded. "I take it that means Willow and Lena?"

"Yes."

"Good. Lena might do her best to pretend otherwise, but they're both good students. And if your skill with elemental magic comes from Freya, a Mermaid and an Elf will be excellent teachers. You know, Freya never got the hang of controlling air until she had a half-Elf tutor. Of course, she and Damon then started sleeping with said tutor, and then she turned out to be a spy..." He sighed before giving me a pointed look.

"Take it from me, Amelia, don't go making your sister's mistakes. If a cute Elf girl offers to help you learn your magic, don't start sleeping with her."

I went bright red.

Willow and I weren't *sleeping* together, but...

Auntie Jess smirked as she turned to Aaron. "Too late. She and Willow are dating. I'm actually shocked that you don't know that, it started before you were cursed."

"Huh," Aaron said, cocking his head to the side in thought. "I must be losing my sneaky spy skills." He then turned back to me. "Well, regardless, if you ever need help with any of your other studies, just let me know. I'll be more than happy to help. I know that part of what drew you to Maria in the first place was that she offered to help tutor you."

I looked away. It sounded almost trivial when he put it like that.

As if the only reason I'd helped her was because she'd offered to teach me after class.

"Speaking of Maria Brown," Aaron continued, and I braced myself, "have you heard anything more from her?"

I shook my head, still not meeting his gaze. "No. Not since she disappeared."

I knew that lying about the bond I had with her was risky, but I also knew that if Aaron found out about it, he would probably want to break it.

My stomach twisted. He was right not to trust her. She did curse him.

But... I really didn't think that she was still manipulating me.

Hell, she was even trying to break the bond herself.

Thankfully, Auntie Jess stepped forward before Aaron could press me further.

"How are you feeling, Amy? About seeing your mother, I mean?"

I shrugged. "Fine, I guess. Why? Has she said anything, or...?"

Auntie Jess gave me a kind smile. "No, she hasn't said anything other than she wants you to meet her at that café in town that you like."

I nodded. It was almost surreal to think about going somewhere as normal as a café after all these weeks.

"But you don't sound fine," Auntie Jess continued. "You sound nervous."

I sighed. "Yeah, okay, I guess I am a little. I just... I have no idea what she's going to say."

"Which is why this will be good for you. It will give you two a chance to clear the air."

I nodded, knowing that she was probably right.

But that didn't make the thought of seeing my mum again any less daunting.

"I already drew a portal for you," Auntie Jess said before looking at the wall behind me.

I followed her gaze to see the portal ready to be activated.

My stomach twisted as I realised that I had been relying on the time it would take her to draw the portal to galvanise myself.

But it looked like I wouldn't have that chance.

My auntie passed me a vial of Faerie dust and I gripped it so hard that my knuckles went white before popping the cork and throwing the glittery dust onto the portal.

The chalk lines on the wall glowed before the glow spread to form a portal.

I bit my lip, my feet refusing to move as a wave of nausea overcame me.

How did I face potential death in the Amazons' trials more easily than this?

My auntie placed a hand on my shoulder, drawing my attention to her worried frown. "Amy, if you don't want to go-"

"No, it's okay. I'm going."

At that, I threw myself through the portal, stumbling into the empty bathroom stall it had deposited me into.

Well, I supposed that was one way of not being seen.

I left the stall and washed my hands – I might not have used the loo, but I'd still had to touch the stall door on the way out – before heading out into the department store in town.

I blinked. When had I last been in town?

In a regular, Human shop?

I pushed that thought aside. As strange as it was, I hadn't missed it.

But I was sure that I would miss Ember Academy if I was forced back here.

That I would miss the one place where I didn't have to hide who I was.

I headed to the café where Auntie Jess had said my mum was waiting, and then hesitated outside the door.

Was she already inside, or should I wait for her out here?

I peered in through the window to see that my mum was already inside, sitting at one of the tables, with two drinks in front of her, along with a millionaire shortbread at the empty seat across from her.

My favourite.

I hesitantly stepped inside the café before heading over to her.

My heart thundered in my chest as she looked up to see me.

No going back now.

I forced a smile, trying to ignore how sweaty my hands were and how light-headed I felt.

I sat down before I could pass out.

"Hi," my mum said after a moment.

"Hi," I managed back.

"I got you your usual drink and cake. I hope that's all right."

"Yeah, it's great." I then lifted the coffee to my lips, more than glad for something to do with my hands.

"Good," my mum said with a small smile before taking a sip of her own coffee. "So, how have you been?"

"Fine," I said between sips of coffee.

'Fine' wasn't exactly accurate, but I didn't think my mum was ready for me to get into my magical problems.

"How are you?" I asked, more out of habit than anything else.

She sighed, looking less than happy.

It took everything I had to keep my expression neutral. I really hoped that she would just say 'fine', like I had.

"It's been difficult," she said, dashing my hopes. "Being on my own, I mean. The house just seems so empty. I knew that you were going to leave home in a couple of years, but I expected your dad to be there with me..."

"I mean, you were the one to kick him out," I muttered into my coffee.

She gave me an unamused look. "After he lied to me about our entire lives."

I put my hand in my pocket and wrapped it around my wand, silently casting a privacy spell.

We needed to talk without worrying.

Though I had never been more grateful for my tendency to cast spells nonverbally than in that moment.

My mum shook her head. "You don't know what it's like, Amy, to wake up and realise that you've spent the last several years having forgotten your daughter."

"No," I agree, "but I know what it's like to realise that you've forgotten a sister."

My mum gave me a sympathetic look. "I wasn't sure that you would even remember. You were so young when she left..."

"I know. And I don't remember her that well, but... I do remember. And I wish that I hadn't forgotten, too."

My mum sighed. "I know that Freya had to make us forget. Your aunt explained that we would have been in danger otherwise, and Freya was only a few years older than you are now when she made that choice. She was scared, and I don't blame her for making the choice that she did. And your aunt... Well, I'm not happy with her, but she understood the danger in telling us the truth. She knew what the consequences might be, and she didn't think it was her place to interfere. And given that she was raised to uphold magical secrecy, even from her own family, I understand why she thought it best to let Freya decide if she would ever return our memories.

"Your father, on the other hand, didn't know that there would be any consequences to telling me the truth when he started to remember, and he wasn't raised to keep magic a secret. He's my husband, Amy, I'm supposed to be able to trust him. But now? How can I ever trust him again? I mean, I wouldn't have kept the truth from him. Would you have, in his place?"

I wanted to give my dad the benefit of the doubt.

I wanted to believe that he had a good reason for doing what he'd done.

But... I couldn't lie, I'd been given the chance to take my mum's memories again, and I'd chosen not to.

I shook my head.

"Exactly," my mum said. "No one would make that choice."

I suppressed a wince, deeply uncomfortable with talking about my dad like this. "Have you tried talking to him about it?"

My mum glared down at her coffee. "I wanted to. I was going to. But then... Did you know that he's moved in with another woman?"

I shifted awkwardly in my seat as I realised why she didn't like the idea of that.

"Auntie Jess said that it was because he didn't do well with being on his own."

My mum just gave me a look and my stomach twisted with guilt.

I hadn't believed that line when Auntie Jess had given it to me, so why was I trying to repeat it now?

I suppressed a sigh.

I was doing it because I didn't want to think about the alternative.

"So... You're not going to try to talk this out with him?" I asked, desperate to change the topic of conversation.

My mum sighed. "I don't know what I'm going to do, Amy." She shook her head. "But enough about me. What about you? I know you said you're fine, but I'm still worried about you being at that school. I understand that you need to learn magic, but your auntie can teach you at home, just like she taught Nightingale."

"That was different, Mum. I'm magically connected to Freya in some way, and it makes my magic different. I need the kind of training I can only get at Ember."

And being connected to Freya puts me in danger, but I decided not to mention that point.

"But what about your friends?" my mum asked. "Wouldn't you rather be back at your old school with them? What about Amanda?"

It took me a moment to realise she meant an old classmate. One I had worked with on a chemistry project, but not really a friend.

Still, she was probably the closest thing I'd had at my old school.

"Actually, I've made some new friends at Ember. They're actually really nice, and no one's been mean to me."

That was technically a lie, but it paled in comparison to the bullying I'd experienced in the past.

My mum looked away, and I got the impression that that hadn't been the answer she'd wanted.

"What about boys?" she eventually said. "You can't really say that you're happy to give up the possibility of dating until university."

I looked down at my coffee.

"I don't care about boys," I eventually settled for saying.

My mum shook her head. "Now, Amy, I know that you've not had luck in the past, but you're too young to be declaring that you're not interested in dating. You just haven't met the right person yet-"

"I have," I said, cutting her off as I realised that she wasn't going to let this go.

Not until I was honest with her.

My heart thundered in my chest, and I could barely hear the ambient noise of the café over my pulse in my ears.

"I'm already dating someone."

I glanced up to see my mum frowning. "You are? Who?"

"A... A classmate of mine. Her name is Willow."

"Oh... She's a... She."

I nodded. "Yeah. I don't care about boys because... Well, because I don't care about them. I never have, really. It just took me a while to realise why..."

"Oh..."

I waited for several moments, wondering if she would say anything else.

She seemed... stuck.

As if she had never once considered this a possibility.

"Well, I... You never seemed..." She waved her hand as if that would help me understand what she was trying to say. "Are you sure?"

I nodded. "Yeah, pretty damn sure."

"Because of this girl? Willow?"

"Well, not just her. She's just... who I'm dating."

"And that's definitely because you want to, not just because there aren't any other options now?"

"Yes," I said, a little sharply. "It's because I want to."

She held up her hands in defence. "All right, I was just asking. It's just... Well, you just know with some kids. But you never seemed gay. I mean, you're not that tomboyish or anything."

"My interests don't dictate who I like."

"Well, no, but you know what I mean."

I sighed. "Kind of. But it still doesn't matter. Whether I seemed gay or not, I am."

"No, I know. I'm just... wrapping my head around it. It's a surprise, that's all."

I nodded, looking back down at my coffee.

I had no idea if she was taking this well or not.

"So... This girl... Willow... Is she nice?"

I nodded again, unable to stop myself from smiling slightly. "Yeah, she is."

"So, you really like her?"

"Yeah, I do."

She nodded. "Okay. Well... It's good that you're happy, I guess."

I ARRIVED BACK AT EMBER Academy to find Willow sitting outside the dormitories, reading a book.

She looked up and smiled slightly as I approached. "Hey, how did it go?"

I sighed. "It was... I don't know. Not as bad as I thought it might be..."

Willow gave me a sympathetic look before standing up and taking my hand in hers.

"Come on," she said. "While you were gone, I went to a ramen place I like and got some to go."

I smiled, having to admit that a single biscuit wasn't enough food for the day. "Thank you."

Willow smiled back as she gently nudged my shoulder with her own. "I was planning to take you there sometime for an actual date, but I figured this would do for now. And maybe we can have that date next weekend. You know, assuming the Slayers don't lock down the school or anything."

My smile turned grim. "I wouldn't rule anything out right now."

"Thankfully, we had this weekend away."

"Yeah," I said, but it was less than enthused.

She gave me another sympathetic look as we reached her room.

On the table by her bed were two cartons with chopsticks resting on top of the plastic lids.

"Where's your roommate?" I asked as Willow closed the door behind us.

"She went home for the weekend, so she won't be back until later tonight. I figured that we could watch movies. You know, if you want."

"Yeah, what movies did you have in mind?"

"Well, why don't we have a look?"

After a brief look through her digital library, we settled on a comedy that we'd both seen plenty of times before.

I didn't have the energy to focus on something new.

"So," Willow said as we both sat next to each other on her bed, eating our ramen and the gyoza she got on the side, the movie having reached an action-sequence we both knew the outcome of, "do you want to talk about how things went with your mum or not?"

I sighed. "She's still upset with my dad for lying to her. Which I totally understand, I just..."

"Wish that they weren't fighting?"

I let out a cold snort. "You know, I can't tell you how many times as a kid I wished they weren't fighting. But now, I would almost prefer that. This isn't fighting, this is just... It's like they've given up. My dad's living with someone else, and my mum... Even if he wasn't living with someone else, I don't think she'd be able to forgive him. I think she wants to try, but... I don't think she could, and I can't blame her for that."

"I'm sure they'll figure out some way to work things out."

I nodded, but I wasn't convinced.

"So, was that the only thing you talked about, or did your mum try to get you to come home again?"

I groaned, leaning back against the wall. "Yeah, she tried to get me to come home again. You know, she tried to use *boys* as an incentive for me to leave the school..."

"Really? What did you tell her?"

"I... I told her that I was already seeing someone."

"Did you specify who that person was? It's okay if you didn't, I just-"

"No, I did," I said, though I couldn't deny that the fact that she wouldn't have pressured me anyway was somewhat of a relief. "I told her about you. And that you're a girl. And that I have no interest in boys."

Willow placed a comforting hand on my arm. "How did she take it?"

"I... I don't know. Well, I think. Or as well as I could have expected. She was... surprised."

"I'm sorry."

I shook my head. "No, it's... Like I said, that's understandable. Of course, she was surprised. It's not like she took it badly."

"Surprise still isn't support."

"It's not *not* support. She just needed a minute. And it least it got her to stop trying to bring me home."

"She was really insistent on that, huh?"

I shrugged. "I think she's lonely. She's not lived on her own for over two decades." I looked down at the last of my ramen. "I told her that I couldn't go home, but I'm not sure that that was the right call... I mean, I know that it's safer for me here, but like I said, she's all on her own after remembering the existence of a daughter who had to leave her behind... Maybe I should go home for a bit to look out for her."

Willow squeezed my arm gently, drawing my attention to the slight frown she was giving me. "Amelia... Going home would put your mum in danger. Whether or not she remains in charge of the Amazons, Dana is still one of the strongest Amazons, and you've pissed her off. Not to mention, if anyone else decided that they wanted to find the truth behind such a powerful Witch... You'll be able to protect her in time, but do you really want to put those skills to the test right now?"

The suggestion that I couldn't handle something stung, but even I wasn't ready to do something suicidal over my pride.

"No, I don't, but that doesn't mean that I feel better about leaving her on her own."

"You know that she's the parent here, right? It's not your job to look out for her."

"I know! I just... That also doesn't make me feel better."

Willow responded by snuggling up to my side. "I'd say your heart is too big, but I have to admit that it's one of the things I like about you."

I couldn't help but smile, a slight blush forming over my cheeks as I put my arm around her, savouring her warmth as I considered just giving up on my food in favour of kisses.

Chapter Five

"You're later than usual."

I shrugged, trying not to grin as I walked around Maria's cauldron, the Witch having another potion brewing.

"I stayed up late watching movies with Willow."

Maria smirked. "Watching movies, huh?"

I glared at her. "Yes, watching movies."

"I may not have picked up everything from this time just yet, Amelia, but I am familiar with the concept of 'Netflix and chill.'"

I placed my hands on my hips, sure that I was bright red. "We kissed. That's it."

And I might have also slipped my hand under Willow's blouse and gotten some rather enticing whimpers out of her for my efforts, but Maria didn't need to know that.

Plus, we'd decided to slow down after that, both of our Energy crackling so much I was almost afraid we'd set the bed on fire.

Maria gave me a look that suggested that she didn't believe me, but she left it alone after that.

"So," she said, "how did seeing your mother go?"

I sighed. "My parents aren't talking to each other and my mum's on her own, and I'm stuck at school because it's too dangerous for me to go home."

"I thought you wanted to stay at the school."

"I do!"

"But you're upset about it?"

I sighed. "My mum's on her own and I don't like leaving her when I could go home."

I expected Maria to say the same thing Willow did. That she was my mother, and I shouldn't have to be the parent here.

But she just nodded in understanding. "Of course. Family can be... tricky."

I raised an eyebrow. "Weren't you the one who was confused about why I was upset that you'd cursed my mother?"

She sighed. "I told you, I'd forgotten what it used to be like. In all honesty... I wanted to forget. Remembering again has been... difficult. As I said, family can be tricky."

I folded my arms. "How was your family tricky?"

"Well, I already told you that I was treated with suspicion for being both powerful and Litcorde. I wasn't allowed to take part in most of the going ons of my coven, which was particularly difficult when my mother was the Coven Head. She already had powerful daughters she expected to take over from her. When my father wanted children, she doubted it would happen. He'd had a wife before her, and they'd never had a child. But even if it did, I would be half-Human, and likely weak enough to be comfortably raised by my father in the Human world.

"Then my father came across an Angel of Life, told her of the problems they were having, and that's how I was born. Too powerful for my mother to ignore, but also born Litcorde.

"I spent my whole childhood thinking that I could please her. If I was just more obedient, if I just proved that I could give a little more of myself, and then a little more, and a little more... I thought that she would change her mind. I thought that I would finally be enough."

She sighed. "But I wasn't. And I couldn't see that until Helena came into my life and convinced me to rebel."

I smiled. "By turning you into an evil mastermind?"

She shook her head. "No, not at all. She really did just want to help. She recognised a kindred spirit in me, and her first suggestion was actually that I try to make a life for myself away from the coven. That I explore my mother's original plan for me to live amongst Humans."

"Oh? How did that go?"

"Well, at first. The village I settled down in welcomed me and my healing knowledge, and after a while, the son of the local chief visited regularly. He was smitten with me, and I saw a real future ahead of me for the first time in my life. A partner, children... A home..."

"So, what happened?"

She shrugged. "He called it off. He said that he fell in love with my beauty, but that I was too cold of a woman to face coming back to every night."

"Ouch," I said, wincing in sympathy.

She shrugged once more. "It... It wasn't the worst thing in the world. I don't think I would have been truly happy with that life."

The room shifted around me, and suddenly, I was holding a goblet of wine and scribbling in a book.

In one of Maria's grimoires.

Writing a curse.

"That'll show them," I slurred. "We'll see how much he likes me when he and his entire village are bleeding from their eyes."

Then two warm hands were around my waist, a head gently resting on my shoulder. "An improvement on my shock curse," a soft voice purred. "I'm impressed. Though, you do realise that it would kill every Human in the village."

"Yeah, well, fuck 'em." I said as I turned around to see one of the most beautiful women I'd ever laid eyes on, with her black hair cropped short to frame her features and piercing red eyes.

She smiled. "I doubt you'll agree in the morning, but I suppose this isn't the worst distraction tonight." She then glanced back to the book. "You know, we make a good team."

"We do. I'm so glad you're here, 'lena."

"Really? Because I was the reason you were ever going to marry him in the first place."

"You're the reason I have the strength to stand on my own. You were right, we make a good team. I don't need him, I don't need any of them. I just need you, here, with me. So, stay. Please. I know you've been thinking about going back to the Underworld, but we both know that you wouldn't be happy there."

She sighed. "I do know that. And I... I was only thinking of going because... Because the thought of you marrying someone else was killing me."

Before I could ask what she meant, she closed the space between us, kissing me.

And it was only a moment before I was kissing her back, my hands on her waist, pulling her close and never letting go.

The world reformed and I saw Maria watching me, her face red.

"Did you just see..."

"The first time you and Helena kissed? Yeah."

"Right... Just kissing?"

I nodded.

"Good. Okay, that's... that's very good..." She shook her head. "And if I needed another reason to stop these memories, I guess I now have it."

I nodded again, having to agree that kissing had been weird enough.

The memories felt so real... I didn't want them to be the first time I experienced anything more than that.

"Regardless," Maria continued, "I know what it is like to have a duty to your family, and I know that you are the kind of person who will uphold that duty, no matter what. But... If those efforts go unnoticed by your family, remember that you have friends who do appreciate you."

She hesitated, and I wondered if she was going to say that I had her as well.

But maybe she felt that that was overstepping.

Or maybe she didn't want to say it if she was planning to break the bond and leave me without her.

But still, I smiled. "Thanks, Maria."

THERE WAS AN ASSEMBLY the next morning, and Natalie and I headed down to the hall, finding Lena, Charlotte and Willow already waiting.

I blushed as I approached Willow, remembering the night before, my Energy crackling just beneath my skin.

Willow gave me a small smile as I stood next to her, a slight blush forming across her cheeks as she reached out her hand to mine.

Her Energy crackled slightly, meeting mine in our palms and I had to stifle a gasp as I realised that her mind was in exactly the same place as mine.

I gulped, doing my best to refocus as Gail stepped onto the stage at the front of the hall, accompanied by a pale, blonde man in heavy armour, his violet eyes hard as he looked over the crowd of students.

"Good morning, everyone," Gail said. "As you all know, the Slayers are here to help us out around the school. It's important for all of you to learn from as many different schools of magical teaching as possible, and the Slayers have offered some of their best instructors to help you over the coming months."

So, she wasn't going to tell everyone that the Slayers were here to investigate the school.

Not that I thought anyone bought it, given how quickly rumours spread here.

No one in the school might have told the students, but many of them had parents involved in the magical community to the extent that they might know the truth.

Gail indicated to the man next to her. "This is Michael. He is the head of the Master Slayers and he shall remain at the school as long as his instructors do, along with a few other Master Slayers. I expect you all to welcome the Slayers, and there is no need to worry about their presence in your classes. They're here to help, and perhaps to learn alongside you."

Gail then stepped aside as Michael stepped forward and cleared his throat.

"I am honoured to have been welcomed to this school and to have the opportunity to help illustrate Slayer values such as strength and discipline to more young minds."

That seemed to be all he had to say, and Gail started clapping.

The rest of us followed, though my claps didn't have heart to them as I turned to my friends.

"'Strength and discipline'?"

Lena shrugged. "Say hello to the alpha-males of the magical world. And prepare to get very tired of it, very quickly."

Charlotte grimaced. "Come on, Lena. I'm sure not all Slayers are bad."

Lena rolled her eyes. "They're like the embodiment of toxic masculinity. I've never met a Slayer who didn't deserve a good kick in the balls."

Natalie turned to her. "Chris didn't seem too bad."

Lena sighed. "Okay, no, he didn't. And if Sarah likes him, then he can't be too bad. You know, assuming that you can ever trust the judgement of a straight woman when it comes to a man."

Charlotte twisted a long lock of chestnut hair between her fingers. "She's not straight."

Lena turned to her with a slight frown. "What?"

"Sarah's not straight. She's on the asexual spectrum."

"Oh, okay. Where did you learn that?"

"It came up during one of my check-ups?"

"Her sexuality came up during one of your check-ups?"

Charlotte looked away, her cheeks turning red. "We were talking about my-" She cut herself off with a sigh. "It doesn't matter. But I trust that Chris is fine, so that means that not all Slayers are bad."

Lena hesitated for a moment, and I got the sense that she was considering backtracking to the thing Charlotte was obviously avoiding.

But then she just sighed. "Okay, well, I suppose he's the one good Slayer, but that doesn't mean I trust the rest of them."

I nodded as I glanced back to Michael.

Something about him unsettled me, but I decided not to say anything.

We already all agreed that we didn't trust the Slayers and adding my bad feeling to the mix seemed more like adding fuel to a fire than anything else.

I HAD HISTORY AS MY first lesson, and I arrived with slight disappointment to see that Mr Stiles wasn't teaching the class.

Of course, he had been a substitute at the beginning of the year, but I had almost been looking forward to being taught by him now that I didn't suspect him of wanting me dead.

I headed to my usual seat and pulled out my tablet, before glancing up to the door as someone else came through.

A rather large, bulky someone with violet eyes.

I suppressed a shiver as the Slayer evaluated the room with a cold, calculating gaze.

"Excuse me," our teacher – Ms Wilson – said from behind the Slayer.

He didn't move and she attempted to squeeze past him, but the Slayer didn't budge an inch.

At least, not for a moment.

Then he finally moved, and my stomach twisted with the realisation that he had done that on purpose.

He'd been trying to intimidate Ms Wilson and possibly the rest of us.

Using this opportunity to show us just how much stronger he was than us.

Either that, or he was just an inconsiderate jerk, but that wasn't much better, and probably stemmed from the fact that he was strong enough to never have to answer to anyone.

The Slayer moved to the back of the class where he stood with his arms folded, his stern gaze fixing on the class.

I felt bad for Ms Wilson, having to take the class with the Slayer watching her.

But then I tried to turn my back on the Slayer, and I struggled, my every instinct telling me not to look away from the potential threat.

I didn't know if Ms Wilson or I had the worst deal, but I did finally force myself to turn to the front of the class.

"Good morning, girls," Ms Wilson said as she picked up a textbook. "You may have noticed that we have a visitor today. Don't worry, he's just here to observe. Now, those of you who were training with the Amazons, you've got a bit of catching up to do, so we'll run through everything you missed today, and if you need more instruction on anything you missed, I'm always available after the school day."

As she went through the topic, I struggled to not keep looking back over my shoulder at the Slayer.

Every moment in the class, my muscles grew tighter, and I could feel him watching me.

After about ten minutes, a girl across the room raised her hand.

"Yes, Claire?" Ms Wilson said.

"I don't feel well, Miss. Can I go to the infirmary?"

Her voice was weak and Ms Wilson frowned as she looked her over.

"You do look pale. Yes, of course, you can go. Does anyone want to volunteer to take her?" She gave Claire a reassuring smile. "I want to make sure you get there safely."

I shot my hand into the air, glad for the chance to leave the room.

Ms Wilson thankfully turned to me with a smile. "Thank you, Amelia. Though, are you sure that you're happy leaving the class when you missed so much while the Amazons were here?"

I nodded. "I'm sure. I'll come back after my final class if I feel I missed too much."

"All right, then."

I got up and made my way over to Claire, trying not to look too taken aback as I got a proper look at her.

She was pale, with dark circles under her eyes.

She pushed herself up from her chair, and I offered out my hand as I realised that she was shaking.

She took it, clinging to my arm in what seemed a desperate attempt to remain upright.

I wasn't sure that she would make it to the infirmary...

Still, we headed out of the classroom, and I did my best to support her as she stumbled.

As we turned a corner, she dropped to her knees, and I barely had time to stop her from hitting the ground as I realised that she had passed out.

"Claire?" I asked, trying to wake her.

She didn't stir.

I frowned. I needed to get her to the infirmary, and fast.

I knew how to heal her when I had plants nearby, but I didn't have any to hand.

I needed to get her to Sarah.

If I didn't...

Before I could complete that thought, the world shifted around us and we were in the middle of the infirmary.

It took me a moment to realise that I had shifted us there in my worry.

I bit my lip. That had been risky. I still didn't have control over my shifting.

But we were both here and Claire seemed intact, if still unconscious.

"Amelia?"

I turned to see Sarah approaching.

"What happened?" she asked.

"Claire said she wasn't feeling well in class. I offered to help bring her here, but she passed out in the corridor, and I shifted us the rest of the way."

Sarah nodded before grabbing Claire and lifting her up onto one of the beds.

"Is she all right?" I asked as Sarah took out her wand and it glowed as she moved it over Claire.

"I'm not sure," Sarah said, frowning. "This isn't any of the usual Human things I would expect from her passing out, and I can't detect any malicious magic on her. Though that doesn't mean that it's not there... Most powerful curses are harder to detect."

"You think this is a curse? Who would attack a student? Maybe Dana or the Slayers?"

Sarah shook her head. "I doubt that it's either of those, Amelia. It's much more likely a prank gone wrong. Or maybe it is a Human illness beyond the obvious. Either way, I have this handled. You should get back to class."

I gave Claire one last look, more than a little worried by how pale she was, but then I nodded, knowing that Sarah didn't need my help to heal someone. I would likely only get in her way.

Chapter Six

"So, have you made any progress?" I asked Maria as I arrived in her tower that night.

"Hmm?" she asked as she raised her head from her book.

"On figuring out how to break our bond. Have you made any progress?"

"No," Maria said with a sigh. "Though you seem more eager than in the past."

I shook my head. "'Eager' isn't the word I would use. More... worried." I shrugged. "I agree that I don't want more of your memories, but I don't really want to stop coming here at night."

Maria gave me a bittersweet smile. "I don't want you to stop coming here, either. But I suspect you won't get rid of one without the other."

I sighed, less than happy with that answer.

"Here," Maria said, handing me one of her tomes. "I'm looking over references to any kind of magical bond to figure out which ones are most similar, so that we can use the untangling method as a base to start from for untangling our bond. I could use another set of eyes."

I took the tome and had to suppress a smile.

As much as I didn't want to untangle our bond, I did appreciate her asking for my help.

I SETTLED BACK INTO the routine of regular classes fairly easily, though I spent the first few moments of every class bracing myself for the arrival of another Slayer.

Thankfully, I got all the way to lunch without seeing one, and by the time I made my way to my next class, I was no longer braced for their presence.

Which resulted in a nasty surprise as I walked into the room, only to see the same Slayer as the day before standing in the corner of the class, watching us all.

It took all of my willpower to tear my gaze from him, trying to focus on anything else.

Thankfully, Willow was already in the class and waiting for me.

I hurried over to her.

"Hey," I said as I approached, breathing a sigh of relief that this class, in focusing on my non-spellcraft magic, gave me a bit of an outlet for riled up Energy. "So, what do you think we should do today?"

Willow tensed, glancing over to the Slayer for just a moment before turning her full attention back to me. "Perhaps we shouldn't use our usual techniques."

It took me a moment to realise what she was saying.

Willow had been helping me to control my Energy with techniques she'd learned from her father.

Her father who was *Fin'Hathan*.

I nodded, figuring that Slayers probably weren't okay with a technique she learned from an assassin.

Even if the technique itself had nothing to do with killing, or even violence.

It was probably less violent than most Slayer training if their heavy muscles and array of weapons were anything to go by.

But I didn't get the impression that the Slayers were above being hypocrites, so sticking to Witch techniques seemed the safer path.

"So," I said, "what do you suggest?"

She sighed. "Well, my next suggestion would be to focus on elemental powers, but..."

I nodded, taking her meaning.

It probably wasn't a good idea to reveal that I was tied to Nature, either.

Which pretty much brought us to the end of what I was supposed to be in this class for...

"Perhaps we could share Energy..." Willow mused. "That's still a Witch technique, and then we can communicate anything else..."

I nodded, taking her meaning.

We could communicate silently through our Energy and then figure something else out.

She sat down cross-legged on the floor before holding her hands palm-side up.

I sat down in front of her and placed my hands on hers.

I allowed my Energy to crackle across my skin to meet hers, and as soon as it did, I gasped with overwhelming feeling.

Usually when we shared Energy, there was only one thing on our minds.

But now?

Now the mix of feelings was like a million different colours of paint being poured over a canvas, moving too fast for me to pick out any individual strand.

I needed to talk to her.

That singular thought burned in me and I moved my Energy as I realised what I needed to do, forming a bridge between us, stronger than what our raw Energy could achieve.

I blinked, as I found Willow and I standing in my room back in the dormitories.

Willow frowned. "Did you shift us here?"

She then moved her hand in front of her, her frown deepening.

"No... This isn't the real world." She turned her attention back to me with a smile. "You drew me into your mind."

I shrugged. "I guess trying to communicate through raw Energy alone was a little overwhelming. It seems like you've got a lot on your mind."

Willow gave me a grim smile. "As do you. The Slayers won't be kind to either of us if they find out our true heritages."

"They really don't like *Fin'Hathan*, huh?"

Willow sighed once more as she made her way to the windowsill and leaned back against it, folding her arms tight across her chest. "The Slayers were built to fight. They were given their magic to protect Humans from Demons, and their entire society is built around facing an enemy head-on. But Elves? Elves are a peaceful people. Pacifists. With one exception."

"The *Fin'Hathan*."

"Exactly. The Slayers don't like pacifists. They don't mesh with their worldview. And the *Fin'Hathan*... They were born because Elves realised that not all violence is direct. And sometimes indirect violence – like refusing to feed another while you let food spoil – becomes a tool of solidifying power. And once that power is solidified, the *Fin'Hathan* are often the best solution to end it. No civilians get hurt if the corrupt people at the top die in their sleep. And if the spectre of the *Fin'Hathan* remains, becoming corrupt loses its lustre."

"But what if the *Fin'Hathan* become corrupt?"

Willow shrugged as she took her dagger from her side, examining the intricate carvings on the blade her father had given her. "Well, that's why they're structured in horizontal cells, all of which answer to their local communities. If one cell loses their way, the others can hold them accountable. It's not impossible that they might become corrupt, but it would be difficult."

"So... If the Slayers don't like Elves because they don't like pacifists, shouldn't they like the *Fin'Hathan*?"

"No. The Slayers would arm every single person so that they can fight the corruption themselves, no matter how bloody it got. No matter how many people would lose their lives. The *Fin'Hathan* exist so that the rest of us don't have to fight. The Slayers see that as a weakness."

I rolled my eyes. "That's because the Slayers are dicks."

Willow smiled as she flipped the dagger from one hand to the other in a startlingly fluid movement. "That they are."

I kept my eyes on the dagger as she twirled it with grace. "You're really good with that, huh?"

Willow took a moment to realise that I was talking about the dagger, her movements had been so absentminded. "Oh, yeah, I guess I am. My father taught me, remember?"

"I remember. I guess I just didn't realise how good you were. I've never seen you in a fight, and then during my final Amazon trials, Lauren-"

Willow gripped the dagger tight, wind swirling around her as her gaze went dark. "Lauren caught me while I was distracted. I shouldn't have let my guard down like that – it was foolish – but..."

She sighed as the wind died down and she put the dagger back in its sheath. "You almost died, Amelia. I was so focused on saving you... I didn't see her until it was too late."

I suppressed a wince as I approached Willow carefully, placing my hand on her arm. "I am so sorry."

She shook her head. "Don't be. They're the ones who should be sorry. They put you through hell, and if I hadn't... If I hadn't been fast enough..."

I nodded, my body bracing for that final hit at the memory of what might have happened if Willow hadn't stopped it.

"I know," I eventually said, my voice sounding hollow, even to my ears.

Willow winced. "I'm sorry. I... I watched as you almost died, but you were the one who... I'm sorry. I should be the one comforting you."

I shook my head. "That was a bad day for both of us. But we're both here and fine, and we can be here for each other."

She unfolded her arms and wrapped her arms around me, holding me tight.

"Why do I get the feeling that you only seem to be dealing with this better than me because you're pushing it down further?"

"Because I have other things to worry about." I pulled away enough to look her in the eye, my hand going to her cheek. "I'd rather look to the future than the past."

"The future where we have to keep hiding? Where no one will accept an Angelborn or *Fin'Hathan*?"

"I thought you weren't planning on following in your father's footsteps."

"I don't think they care."

"What about if Esme wins this election? She might change things..."

"I want to believe that. I really do. But she's going to be up against so much, and there's no guarantee that the covens will listen to her the same way that they listen to Dana. And even if she takes over, I don't think she can reverse Dana's decision not to allow me to join the Amazons again. So, there's a chance that even if she wins, neither she nor the covens will take me."

I sighed. "Yeah... I know what you mean. I've been worried about the same thing. Though..."

"Though?"

"Maria has pointed out that there's nothing stopping us from making our own secret community of Witches if we wanted. One that isn't beholden to the Amazons or the Council of Light like the school is."

Willow frowned. "That sounds... amazing. But a project like that... The Amazons and the Council of Light won't allow it. It would threaten their power. If you want to build something like that, you would have to defend it."

"I know. Which is why I've been trying not to give her idea much thought. It's... exhausting. But if you were with me..."

She smiled. "It becomes less exhausting?"

I nodded.

She leaned forward and captured my lips in hers.

I melted into her embrace, my hands at her waist gripping her blouse as I found myself gripped by a desperate desire to remove it.

And just as I had that thought, the fabric melted away from beneath my hands, leaving Willow in nothing but her bra as she pulled away our kiss, more than a little breathless.

"Careful," she said. "We're in your mind. Whatever you think will become reality."

My cheeks flushed. "Sorry. I didn't realise."

"I don't mind. Though, it is a little unfair..."

At that, she moved to unbutton my own blouse, slowly revealing the simple white t-shirt bra beneath.

I felt my face heat further as I realised that I should have perhaps imagined something a little more adventurous than my usual underwear.

Would I look totally unprepared when she reached the white cotton knickers?

Of course, that would only happen if she had the intention of going that far, and I found my breath hitching in my throat at the thought.

It wasn't real, I knew that, but it certainly felt real...

It felt real, and I never wanted this feeling to stop. The warmth that spread through me, almost bringing tears to my eyes.

Maybe we could do this, if we were together.

Maybe we could build a place for people like us when we graduated.

Maybe we could have a home.

Together.

I wanted that, I realised.

I wanted somewhere to call home, and I wanted it to be with Willow. For this loving warmth to never fade.

Because that's what it was, I realised. Where this feeling came from...

Love.

I was in love with Willow.

Head over heels, could barely breathe at the thought, *love.*

Every cell of my body sang with the truth of the thought as Willow finally finished unbuttoning my shirt, leaning in close for another kiss.

But I placed my hand on her cheek, pausing her.

"Willow, I..."

My words died in my throat.

Willow had said that magical beings feel more strongly than Humans.

That's why we were taking things slow, that's why we hadn't been this undressed with each other in the real world yet.

What if telling her that I loved her caused her to back away again?

To slow down, out of fear that we were rushing into things.

And maybe we were. Maybe it was just my magic, and the fact that we'd been through so much together in such a short time, and then my ADHD did make me impulsive and bad at regulating my emotions...

Shit, what if it wasn't just my magic? What if I'd fallen so hard for her because my brain was wired to go fast and intense?

What if she didn't feel the same way?

Sure, she liked me, but this... This was *more.*

What if I told her and it freaked her out?

What if she thought I was clingy and weird?

Willow's hands played with the edges of my shirt as she patiently waited for me to find my words.

But then her gentle, fluid motions became shaky.

"Willow?" I asked, looking down at her shaking hands just a moment before she fell to her knees.

And then we were back in the classroom, sitting exactly where we had before.

"Are you okay?" I asked. "Is something wrong?"

"I... I'm not sure. I feel... dizzy and faint."

Willow's hand went to her head and I realised how pale she looked. Just like Claire had.

I jumped up and looked to Miss Tilly.

"I need to get Willow to the infirmary. Quickly."

Miss Tilly nodded with a worried frown as she saw the state Willow was in. "Of course."

At that, I helped Willow to her feet and she leaned against me.

"You'll be all right," I promised her, hoping with everything I had that I wasn't lying.

Willow only managed a weak nod as we made our way through the corridors.

I bit my lip as she stumbled, hoping that I wouldn't have to risk shifting her.

Thankfully, we reached the infirmary, but with only just enough time for Sarah to help me catch Willow as she fainted.

"She's sick," I said as I helped Sarah get her to an empty bed. "She got so pale so suddenly... It was just like Claire."

Sarah nodded with a grimace as we settled Willow onto the bed. "She's not the only one."

At that, I looked around the infirmary to see that Willow was the fifth unconscious student in the room.

And Claire was still there.

"What's wrong with them?" I asked. "Some kind of magical illness?"

Before Sarah could respond, a new voice boomed through the room. "That was exactly what I was about to ask."

I looked up to see Michael striding in, with Gail struggling to keep pace beside him.

Gail glared at him as he finally stopped next to us.

"Michael, as much as I am glad for your help, you are here to observe. You cannot do that unless you let me do my job."

He fixed her with a hard look, and I thought for a moment that he was going to argue, but then he nodded and stepped back.

Gail then sighed as she looked at Willow before turning to Sarah and signing as she spoke. "Another student? That's five now. Do you have any idea what's causing it?"

Sarah shook her head, signing as well. "I don't have a clue. It doesn't look like any sickness or curse I've ever seen. It almost looks as if something is draining their life force, but I can't sense the life force actually leaving. There's no clear trail to follow."

"And is there any connection between the students? Any way this might have spread?"

"It's a school, Gail. They're not classmates, and none of them share a room, but that doesn't mean that they didn't pass in the hallways or eat lunch near each other. But that's assuming it spreads like an illness. If it's a curse, that's more likely to be personal."

Gail groaned, pinching the bridge of her nose. "And to my knowledge, there aren't any social connections between the girls, and they don't have enemies. Willow, for example, is quiet and keeps to herself. It could be motivated by bigotry, but three of the other girls are pureblooded Witches.

"Well, until we learn how this spreads, we should quarantine the school. I'll let the students know, and keep me informed if you learn anything else or need any help. Feel free to pull staff with healing abilities, like Aaron, from their regular duties."

Sarah nodded as Gail turned to leave.

Michael didn't follow her, instead scrutinising Sarah and me for a moment.

Gail waited for him, and just before it seemed that she was going to remind him to leave, he turned and stormed from the room, with Gail struggling to keep up once more.

I turned my attention to Willow and took her hand in mine.

"You won't go back to class if I tell you to, will you?"

I looked up to see Sarah giving me a sympathetic look.

I shook my head.

"Okay. But you can't stay here overnight, and you will need to be back in classes tomorrow."

I wasn't happy with that, but I nodded, figuring that arguing wouldn't help.

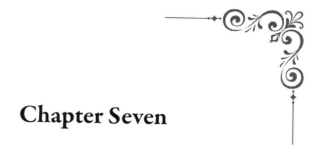

Chapter Seven

I rushed over to Maria as soon as I arrived in her tower that night. "There's something wrong at the school."

Maria frowned as she looked up from her book. "Something besides the Slayers?"

I nodded. "Students are dropping unconscious, but no one can figure out why."

Maria sighed. "I will help you as much as I can, but you know that I'm not skilled with healing magic."

I tried not to look too crestfallen at the reminder.

I was so used to turning to Maria with my magical problems, I'd forgotten that even she had holes in her knowledge.

"There might be something I can do for now," Maria said. "I've yet to find a way to break this bond, but I have learned more about it, and I think that I can use it to cast a protection spell on you. Hopefully, whatever is happening at the school won't be able to affect you with it in effect."

"Could I use the same spell on other students? To inoculate them before they're affected?"

"I doubt it. It's going to take some rare ingredients that I doubt the school carries. With the Vulcan Plains cut off, I probably have one of the only supplies of Dragon blood left, and I don't have much. Protecting you is going to use up most of it."

I nodded. I didn't like that I wouldn't be able to protect my friends, but at least I wouldn't have to worry about getting sick while I helped to figure out what was wrong.

Assuming that I could help.

And assuming that this protection spell worked...

Maria quickly threw together some ingredients in a flask before lighting a ring of candles at her desk and then pulling her wand out and drawing a rune on the table.

Once she was done, she turned to me.

"Here, give me your hand."

I nodded, heading over to her.

"The left one, where the scars are worst."

I held out my hand and she took it, holding it over the rune with one hand as she picked up the flask with the other and poured it onto the rune.

The rune lit with bright pink flames, though they didn't burn as they reached my hand.

No, they poured up, into my skin, causing my scars to glow.

I felt the magic surge through me, strengthening me.

Once the spell was complete, Maria let go of my hand and turned to me with a slight frown.

"Something wrong?" I asked.

"No, just... Your scars."

I looked down at them and realised that they had eased slightly.

"So, what?" I said. "The protection spell healed me? Did it weaken the bond?"

"It shouldn't have. In all honesty, I was worried that it would strengthen it. But given the danger at the school, that seemed the smaller risk."

I turned to her bookshelf and sighed as I realised that her worry hadn't been for nothing. "The first five tomes are ones you took from your mother's coven when you left. The next three are from Helena, then you wrote the next two, and then the next four were from Helena again."

I turned back to see that Maria's frown had deepened. "Did you get another flash of memory?"

"No, I just knew it."

"Then we really need to break this bond. I have centuries of memories, and you only have sixteen years. I'm worried that if you remember too much..."

I shuddered as I followed her train of thought. "If I remember too much, I might end up more you than me."

She nodded. "How do you feel?"

I frowned as I focused inwards. "It didn't feel as intrusive as the last few times. And it's not the same as my own memories. It's more like something I read in a book. I know it, but it doesn't feel like I lived it."

"For now. But I don't want to test that." Maria sighed. "But let me focus on the bond. You should focus on what's happening at the school. And while I might not be able to help you, you've had success in the past with using your tie to Nature as a way to access healing magic."

"Yeah, I guess I have..."

"Do you know which of my books have information on Nature? If not, I'll help you find them before I return to my research on the bond."

"I think I know where to look."

I GROANED AS I AWOKE the next morning, feeling anything but rested.

Whenever I spent a long night with Maria, I struggled to feel as if I'd gotten a good night's sleep.

I probably didn't. My brain probably didn't get the chance to rest.

And that wasn't helped by me spending all night feverishly researching.

Trying to find some way – any way – to wake up Willow.

"Are you okay?" Natalie asked, and I turned to her as I sat up to see that she was already up and reading on her phone.

"Yeah," I said.

Natalie gave me a disbelieving look as she got out of her own bed and came to sit on the edge of mine.

"Really? Because if my girlfriend was unconscious and no one knew how to wake her…"

I cringed. "Yeah, I guess I'm not 'okay'. But it's fine. I just… I just need to figure out how to wake her up."

"If anyone can, it's you." Natalie then reached over and placed a comforting hand on my arm. "And I'm here for you. I'll help in any way that I can."

I managed a watery smile, her words meaning more than I suspected she knew. "Thank you, Natalie. Really. I appreciate it."

IT WASN'T JUST NATALIE who offered to help. Charlotte and Lena also chimed in with their intention to help me find a cure as soon as Natalie and I arrived at breakfast.

It was almost daunting how quickly everyone assumed that I would be trying to help find a cure.

I was glad that my friends had faith in me, but I kind of wished that someone else would take the lead on this.

But then, if they did, I knew that I would be pestering them every five minutes anyway, wanting to make sure they were doing it right, so maybe it was better this way.

We headed to the library at break and took out every book that could possibly help and piled them up on the table.

We didn't have long, but we could make a good start and come back at lunch.

"All right, so, 'Understanding Magical Energy Flows: A Beginner's Guide to the Magical Currents that Control Our World' sounds promising, right?" I asked, reading the spine of one of the books as I picked it up.

Lena rolled her eyes. "It sounds like someone didn't know how to succinctly title a book."

Charlotte nodded. "Or write one. I've tried to get through that one before and it's a slog. But... you're right, it might help."

Natalie reached her hand out. "Give it to me. Vampire speed will hopefully compensate for tedious writing."

I smiled as I handed it over, glad that I wouldn't have to deal with it.

I returned my attention to the pile, but before I could find another book, someone cleared their throat.

I looked up to see a couple of girls approaching. I didn't recognise either of them well enough to know their names, but I had seen them around school.

"Are you trying to find a way to help the sick Witches wake up?" one of them asked. "I heard that Willow was one of the girls affected. I'm sorry."

"Thank you," I managed, barely able to remember the appropriate response through the ache in my heart. "And yes, we are trying to find some way to help."

"Want a hand? We... We're sick of waiting around for Claire to get better."

"Yeah, sure," I said.

"Thanks. There are a few others who might be interested. Do you mind if I message them?"

"No, go right ahead."

A snort came from behind us and I turned to see two Slayers standing by the door.

They didn't look any older than us, and I presumed they were trainees that the Slayers had brought with them.

I placed my hands on my hips and glared at them. "Got something to say?"

One of them was leaning against the wall, and he pushed off from it before sauntering over with a smug look that made me want to punch his face into next week. "We were bored and wondered where everyone was. It looks like everyone's pathetically moping. Except for you, turning to books to fight your battles." He snorted again, shaking his head. "I honestly don't know which of you Witches are more pathetic, to be honest."

I raised an eyebrow. "You're starting on me because I'm dealing with a magical illness or curse by... doing research? What would you do? Punch the curse?"

"If you weren't seen as weak, you wouldn't be a target of such attacks. And clearly those who succumbed to the curse are the weakest among you. Like that half-Elf girl..."

I clenched my teeth as Dark Energy crackled just beneath my skin.

"I'll show you just how weak Witches are," I growled.

The Slayer smiled. "By all means."

He stepped outside and I barrelled after him, barely hearing Natalie call my name.

I went to strike him hard with Dark Energy, but he dodged out of the way of my blast, moving faster than I could see.

Before I had a chance to recover from letting loose such a heavy blast of my magic, the Slayer was next to me, his fist pounding my gut.

I dropped to the ground, the wind knocked out of me.

I coughed, desperately trying to regain my breath before the Slayer could literally kick me while I was down.

I desperately grabbed my wand, focusing on a protection spell as I cursed myself for forgetting it in my haste.

The Slayer tried to kick me, but the spell repelled his foot as I gathered enough breath to clamber to my feet.

He snorted once more. "You think that little shield is going to stop me?"

He lifted his hand and it crackled with lightning.

Not Energy, but electricity.

He thrust his hand forward and I cried out as my shield almost immediately broke under the impact and the lightning hit me.

Dark Energy surged over my skin at the pain, and I hurled it out to hit him once more.

He was so wrapped up in his own attack that my blast hit him, causing him to stop and stumble back.

I immediately pounced on the tiny advantage, launching myself at him and striking him hard enough to keep him stumbling.

I went to strike again, hoping to knock him to the ground, but he managed to recover enough to grab my fist in his hand.

I cried out with pain as he twisted my hand back, bending my arm in such a way that I was forced to my knees to stop my arm from breaking.

"Stop!"

Natalie rushed between us, knocking the Slayer back with her Vampire strength.

"That's enough," she said as she glared at the Slayer. "What happened to you all just being here to learn?"

"There is nothing you weaklings could teach us. And before you blame me for this fight, remember that your friend threw the first punch."

"Only after you rubbed salt in the wound of her girlfriend being in the infirmary. You knew exactly what you were doing. You knew that you could provoke a fight."

The Slayer just shrugged, and Natalie turned to me. "Come on. We should get Sarah to look at your wounds."

"I'm fine," I said quickly, not wanting to go to the infirmary.

Not wanting to see Willow lying there, lifeless...

"No, you're not."

The look in Natalie's eyes told me that she wasn't going to back down, so I reluctantly nodded and followed her away from the others and towards the infirmary.

Mr Stiles was leaving as we arrived.

"Amy," he said as he saw me. "Is something wrong?"

Natalie folded her arms. "She got into a fight with a Slayer."

"He was being a dick," I added, not wanting it to sound like I'd just attacked him for no reason.

Mr Stiles sighed as he approached me. "Here, let me get a look at you."

"I was going to take her to Sarah," Natalie said.

"I'm a healer as well," Mr Stiles said. "And Sarah's busy trying to find a cure to whatever's wrong with the other students. Probably best not to bother her over a scuffle."

Mr Stiles looked me over before shrugging. "You're fine, Amy. A little bruised, but you'll live. I'll grab you a healing potion and that will sort you out."

I nodded. "Thanks."

He then looked me over again before sighing and folding his arms. "I would tell you to try to avoid the Slayers from now on, but I get the feeling that you're too much like your sister to ever back down from a fight."

I shifted my weight awkwardly, not sure how to respond.

"Well, if you're going to keep throwing yourself into danger, I should probably teach you how to not get beaten so bad."

"I already have a Magical Self-Defence teacher."

"I know, but I think you need something a little more than two one-hour sessions a week. Especially with those scars of yours. You're lucky the Slayer didn't hit them."

I nodded as I looked down at the scars in question. I'd actually been having a pretty good day with them, and when I looked closer, they seemed just like they had in my dream, after Maria had cast the protection spell.

Not healed, but slightly less raw.

"If you want, I can meet you tonight after your last class and see if I can't help you get to the point where you no longer have to worry about Slayers beating you in a fight."

I nodded. "I'd like that."

"All right. I'll be back out in a moment with your potion."

He headed back into the infirmary and Natalie made her way over to me.

"Are you sure you're all right?"

"You heard Mr Stiles. I'm fine."

"I didn't mean physically. Amy, you had to know that that Slayer would beat you in that fight. You're good, but you're not that good. And yet you charged in anyway."

I shrugged, looking away. "It's like you said, he riled me up on purpose, and I just... I just saw red."

"Because you're worried about Willow?"

I shrugged again. "I guess..."

"We'll figure this out, Amy. It's only been a day."

"I know, I just... When the Amazons almost killed me, she was there to save me, along with you and the others. But she... She was hurt, and she lost her chance to ever join the Amazons. She sacrificed a lot for me, and now I need to return the favour. I owe it to her. And... And even if I didn't, I can't lose her, Nat."

Those last words came out as nothing more than a whisper and Natalie gave me a small, understanding smile.

"I know. But drawing the Slayers' attention to you won't help her. All you'll do is make it harder for you to help her."

"I... I know, I just..."

"You're feeling too much and need an outlet?"

I nodded, biting my lip.

She sighed. "I know the feeling. When I first tasted blood... It was overwhelming. And then when I realised what I'd done – that I'd bitten my friend – it was just too much. I think I cried for days. But you're not really much of a crier, huh?"

"I used to be. Until I realised just how much people will bully you for that."

"Well, hopefully, training with Mr Stiles will give you an outlet. But if you need to talk, I'm here."

I smiled and nodded as she placed a reassuring hand on my arm.

Her touch was cool, but that didn't stop my skin from flooding with warmth at the gesture.

But then the door to the infirmary opened, and she pulled away as Mr Stiles stepped through.

"Here," he said, passing me a healing potion. "That should help."

"Thanks," I said before downing the potion and easing my pain.

Though not by nearly enough.

THE BELL RANG BEFORE I got back to the library, but we were all back there at lunch, along with a dozen other girls.

Not that that was much help as the pile of read books grew larger and larger, and we were no closer to finding an answer.

I turned to Charlotte as I realised that there was only five minutes left before we had to be back in classes. "What have we got so far?"

She sighed as she picked up the list of possible leads we'd put together. "Various stories about Angels of Life being asked to cure illness, though most seem to be tales about how they won't interfere in the natural course of events; details on how Demon nobles inoculate themselves against magical illnesses, but they come with warnings that they wouldn't work with other species as well as evidence that it doesn't actually work as well as they claim, they just hide when it doesn't; and a story about a Daughter of Nature healing a village from a plague by appealing to her mother."

"Wait, what was that last one? That sounded promising."

"I thought so too before I remembered that Nature only talks to her Daughters. We would need a Daughter of Nature to appeal to her, and the only one alive is Queen Freya. And maybe Princess Katherine, but she's too young to have come into her magic yet. Either way, the Daughter acted as the tether between the village and her mother. The only way for Queen Freya to do that would be for her to break quarantine and come here. No one is going to allow that. It's too dangerous."

I groaned, knowing that she was right.

"Okay, well, let's just keep going."

I HAD TO FORCE MYSELF to leave the library to head to my afternoon lessons, and it was a struggle to concentrate on anything other than the fact that Willow and the others were still lying in the infirmary, and no one had any idea of how to help.

But if anything – aside from finding the answer and everyone waking up – was going to help, it would be getting some training in how to kick a Slayer's arse.

So, I ignored the urge to follow my friends to the library after my final class, and instead headed to Mr Stiles' room.

"Ah, Amelia. Here for some training?"

"Yeah," I said. "Assuming it's still fine, and Sarah doesn't need you for anything..."

He shook his head. "Everything is stable in the infirmary, and Sarah's at that point where I think I was more in her way than helping. I'll check back with her tomorrow, but for tonight, I'm sure that I'll be better off teaching you. So, how's your shifting?"

I cringed. "I've done it a couple of times, but never where I've really been in control of it."

"Do you think you could try to shift to the gym?"

"What are the chances of me shifting myself into the wall?"

"Less if you don't think about it."

I wasn't sure if he was joking or not, so I just nodded before closing my eyes and picturing the gym, trying to remember what it had felt like the last time I shifted.

As if the world was slipping out from under me.

I stumbled and opened my eyes, seeing that we were in the empty gym.

Mr Siles then appeared next to me with a smile. "Well, it looks like you've got the hang of it. Though be careful. The further you try to go, the harder it is. And it drains your magic as much as anything else, so you can exhaust yourself."

I nodded. "I'll be careful."

"Then I guess we should get started." He opened his arms wide. "Try to come at me. I want to see how good you are."

I grimaced, knowing that I was okay, but also knowing that Mr Stiles had been chosen as one of my sister's guards.

I guessed it took more than a few years of Taekwondo to get that job.

Still, I raised my hands before doing as Mr Stiles said and heading right for him.

He blocked my first strike but didn't respond.

No, he let me strike, and strike again.

I realised that he was letting me continue so that he could get an idea of my skills.

Not that they were particularly impressive, as he kept blocking any attempt to attack him.

Then he struck, his palm hitting hard against my scars and causing me to double over with blinding pain.

"Fuck," I spat, forgetting that I was talking to a teacher. "What the hell did you do that for?"

Thankfully, he didn't chastise me for my outburst.

"I did that because it's the first thing that any savvy opponent will do in a fight. As soon as they realise that you've got a weakness, they'll attack it."

"Yeah, thanks," I managed between pained gasps. "I already knew that. I didn't need the vivid reminder."

"I know, but this wasn't just a reminder. Do you feel that?"

"Feel what?"

"Dark Energy. You're practically bursting at the seams with it."

I nodded. I'd gotten so used to burying the feeling, so scared I would hurt someone like I hurt Mr Stiles when I first broke through, that I barely noticed it anymore.

But now that Mr Stiles had pointed it out, I could feel the Energy crackling under my skin, begging for release.

"Sorry," I managed through gritted teeth, the Energy growing stronger the more I worried about it. "I'm trying to hold it back..."

"I don't want you to hold it back, Amelia. I want you to unleash it."

I frowned. "Don't you remember what happened when I broke through?"

"Yes, you threw me clean across the corridor."

"So why would you want me to do that again?"

"It's not that I want you to hurt me now, it's that I want you to hurt someone else if you get into a fight in the future. Not every fight will be a schoolyard scrap, Amelia. And even those are dangerous where Slayers are involved.

"I understand that you don't want to hurt me, but I can take it, and you need to practice. You need to learn to control it. Witches won't teach you that. They don't use their raw Energy in a fight. But Demons do. We harness our pain and turn it into strength."

He looked me up and down. "It looks like you've been practicing control of your raw Energy in order to suppress it, but do you have enough control to manipulate it? To direct it where you need it most?"

My thoughts went to my Energy training with Willow.

The way she would gently guide my Energy, allowing me to feel it, and then control it on my own.

Dark Energy cascaded through me as my heart ached in my chest at the reminder of my girlfriend.

But I reigned it in.

And held it tight.

Mr Stiles didn't look happy, though, as he regarded me softly. "What were you thinking about to produce that much Dark Energy just now?"

"Willow," I admitted through clenched teeth.

"You really love her, don't you?"

I didn't respond.

I knew that he was right, but saying it aloud...

"She'll be okay," Mr Stiles said. "She'll recover."

"Why are you trying to cheer me up? Don't you want me to use my raw Energy?"

"Yes, but I also don't want you to exhaust yourself. But now that you're all juiced up, I want you to take that Energy and focus it into your muscles. Give them the strength to move faster and hit harder."

I nodded, doing as he said and directing my Energy where it needed to go.

It flooded through my body and I felt almost uncomfortably warm.

But then, I supposed that I was essentially overclocking myself with no way to upgrade my cooling system.

"Now," Mr Stiles said, "attempt to strike me again."

I nodded before leaping into action.

I moved faster than my mind could keep up with, only muscle memory stopping me from stumbling as I struggled to keep up.

But the rush of adrenaline coursing through me triggered my hyperfocus, and my mind finally caught up with my movements, allowing me to finally get past Mr Stiles' blocks.

I struck him hard in the chest, sending him stumbling back, and I stopped, worried that I'd hurt him.

Thankfully, he smiled as he righted himself. "That would have knocked that Slayer boy to his knees. Your scars might hurt if they get hit, but if you can channel that pain into ending the fight with your next blow, it's not so bad."

I nodded. "Yeah, I guess not."

"All right. Ready to go another round?"

I nodded again as I slowed down, my Energy waning, and we went back to sparring at regular speed.

Mr Stiles got through my defences again, but as soon as he hit my scars, I channelled my pain and surprise into my muscles, slipping away from his next strike and then striking him in the chest once more.

He flew through the air, landing with a thump.

"Sorry," I squeaked as I hurried over, finding my muscles sluggish to respond as exhaustion started to set in.

As I got closer, I realised that his clothing was singed around where I'd hit him.

He pushed himself into a sitting position, coughing slightly as I kneeled next to him.

"No need to apologise," he said with a grin. "That was quite the display. You should be proud. It's not easy to knock me down."

I bit my lip, wanting to take the compliment, but feeling that it was perhaps too easy. "Were you fighting at full power?"

He sighed, shrugging slightly. "Okay, I guess not. But this was your first training session. And this was a good start."

"We should go again, but don't limit yourself this time."

He raised an eyebrow. "How are you feeling?"

I was about to say 'fine', but I found myself unable to as I tried to stand up, and stumbled, feeling light-headed.

"You've exhausted yourself," Mr Stiles said as he got to his feet. "This is probably the best technique to keep you safe in a life-or-death situation, given your scars, but it's not without downsides. Using raw Energy like that will exhaust you quickly. Even the strongest Demons struggle with it."

I looked away, less than happy with that assessment.

I had no idea why the Slayers were here, but if this turned into a fight, I had to be ready.

"You'll get better in time," Mr Stiles said and I looked to meet his gaze, seeing that he was giving me a reassuring smile, "but it's something you need to build up over time, and all exhausting yourself today will do is mean that you can't train tomorrow."

I sighed. "Yeah, okay."

"So, I'll see you back here tomorrow after school?"

"Yeah, I'll be back."

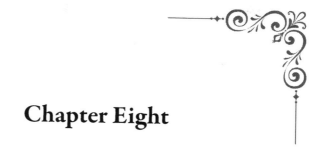

Chapter Eight

I immediately rushed over to Maria's books when I arrived in her tower that night, but I found that the ones I had been reading were gone.

I turned to where Maria was sitting in the corner, about to ask where they were, only to see her reading and taking studious notes.

I approached, and she didn't look up until I got close and then placed my hand in front of the book she was reading.

She looked up with a start. "Amelia!" She then sighed, leaning back in her chair and pushing her hair out of her face. "You seemed very upset about Willow, so while I'm not good at healing magic, I thought I could at least help with your research."

"Have you found anything?" I asked, almost bouncing with anticipation.

She sighed. "I wish that I could say that I have even a lead on a cure, but I can't seem to find any reference to this kind of disease or curse. Or rather, I've found lots of references, but I don't know enough about what's happened to Willow to narrow it down. Has Sarah found out anything else?"

I sighed, leaning back against Maria's desk. "Not that I've heard, but I haven't spoken to her. She's been so busy with treating the students... But Mr Stiles has been working with her, and he didn't say anything during training."

She raised an eyebrow. "Training?"

"Yeah," I said, folding my arms. "He's trying to help me get better at fighting."

Her gaze grew darker. "I was afraid you were going to say that..."

"Why? You don't approve?"

"Oh, I approve of you learning to fight, and Aaron is probably the best teacher for you, but it's clear that your sister wants him to keep you safe, and it's also clear that Aaron has always taken that to mean keeping you away from danger. If he's teaching you to fight, that means that he no longer sees that as a possibility. And from an optimist like him, that's quite the assessment..."

I bit my lip, not wanting to admit that she was right, but knowing that she probably was. "Well, he is teaching me to fight now, so I'll be able to take care of myself."

Maria nodded, though she didn't seem convinced.

She looked back at her book, and I almost expected her to start catastrophizing about my situation, but instead she said, "We need to know more about what's happening to Willow and the others before we can narrow our search. When researching how to remove our bond, I think I found something that might help. A way to enter the mind of someone under an intense curse. The spell is supposed to be used to get information out of an enemy you've cursed and can't risk waking up, but it's not invasive. Not beyond your presence in their mind, and I doubt Willow will mind your presence. Especially not when you're there to help her."

I frowned. "What do you think I'll find in her mind? I mean, Willow didn't know anything about what was going on before she was cursed."

"No, but Willow is a gifted Witch. She can likely sense what's happening to her, and that might mean that she can give you a perspective that you can't get from the outside. Hopefully, she can help you figure out how to heal her."

"Okay then. Show me what I need to do."

I BOLTED OUT OF BED as soon as I woke up, grabbing my clothes and getting dressed.

I needed to stop by the infirmary before classes.

I couldn't leave this until later.

Natalie was in the bathroom, so I just got dressed and headed out.

I could always come back to use the loo and brush my teeth later.

I practically sprinted down to the infirmary and then slipped inside.

I realised as I made my way through the door that I didn't have an excuse for what I was doing there, and Sarah hadn't exactly been happy the last time Maria had tried to help me.

But as I entered, I saw that Sarah was more than busy at the other end of the room, with Aaron and Auntie Jess.

No one looked my way as I entered, but my hand instinctively went to my wand and I cast a slight glamour over myself, making me blend with the shadows as I made my way around the edge of the room to where Willow was lying.

Gail sighed as I walked, and my ears couldn't help but prick up.

"And there's really nothing more you can tell me?" she asked Sarah, speaking with her hands as much as her voice.

Sarah shook her head. "I wish that I had more for you, but every test I've run so far has come up negative. I simply cannot find the source of whatever's draining them."

"But you are sure that something's draining their lifeforce?"

"Yes. Nothing else makes sense with their symptoms, but it's strange, it's almost stable. It takes enough lifeforce to keep them unconscious, but it never takes enough to kill them."

"At least until it hits someone whose lifeforce is already weakened."

"Do you have any students like that?"

"I don't think so, but you can never be certain."

Auntie Jess shifted her weight from one foot to the other. "I can brew protective potions and put them in the food, but that won't slow whatever this is. It will just protect anyone who can't survive what's already affecting these students."

"That's still better than nothing." Gail then turned back to Sarah. "I should leave you three to your work. Let me know if anything changes."

"Of course," Sarah said, and Gail headed for the door, though as she reached it, she stumbled, grabbing the wall to keep herself upright.

Auntie Jess hurried over to her, helping her stay upright as she gave her a concerned frown. "Gail..."

"I'm fine," Gail tried to say. "It's just a lack of sleep. Or stress with the Slayers being here. That's all."

Sarah made her way over to them and pulled out her wand.

After a quick examination, she gave Gail an apologetic look. "No, it's not. Whatever is draining the lifeforce of the students is targeting you as well now."

"I'm not a student, I'll be able to keep going."

"You're strong, Gail, but not that strong. Come on, you need to sit down."

Gail gave her a defiant look, though it crumbled as she swayed, and it became clear that Auntie Jess was the only thing keeping her upright.

Auntie Jess led Gail down to one of the empty beds, and Gail didn't fight her, though I wasn't sure if that was because she didn't want to or because she couldn't.

Gail gripped Jess' arm tight as she sat down on the bed.

"You cannot let the school collapse without me," she said. "You can't let the Slayers use this to shut it down."

Auntie Jess struggled to meet her gaze. "Gail... You have other teachers. Better teachers."

"No one I trust as much as you. Jessica, if you don't take the job now, Michael will try to take charge of the school. You cannot let him."

"I... You're sure that you want me as your deputy? Over anyone else?"

"That's what I've been saying for months."

Auntie Jess bit her lip, but then nodded. "Okay, fine. But as soon as this crisis is over, you have to pick someone better qualified."

"Jessica, if you get the school through this crisis, no one will be more qualified."

Auntie Jess smiled at that, though her smile didn't last long, as Gail slumped forward in her arms, out cold.

Sarah helped Auntie Jess to lie Gail down and Auntie Jess took Gail's hand for a moment and squeezed before letting go and turning to the others in the room.

She still hadn't seen me.

"Don't tell anyone what happened here. I want to talk to the rest of the staff before the Slayers realise what's happened and try to take control of the school."

Sarah and Mr Stiles nodded, and I had to stop myself from speaking up.

From offering my help.

But the best way to help would be to figure out what's happening to everyone and figuring out how to stop it.

So, I turned my attention to Willow and the spell Maria had taught me the night before.

I took Willow's hand in mine, while my other hand grasped my wand as I recited the incantation in my mind.

I closed my eyes to focus, and when I reopened them, I was standing in the middle of a field.

Behind me was a large farmhouse, with charms around the door.

A coven, I supposed.

I hadn't put much thought into how covens actually worked, but I supposed that they would have to be in large buildings to accommodate so many Witches.

My attention was drawn back to the field by a grunt of effort, and I turned to see Willow darting out of the way of a dagger.

I followed the path the dagger must have taken to see an older man, with long white hair tied back away from his pointed ears.

An Elf.

Her father, if I were to guess.

"Silence is paramount," Willow's father said, and I realised that the grunt had come from her.

"You almost got me that time!"

"Then don't let me get you."

He lunged at her, and Willow launched herself into the air, the wind propelling her and allowing her to flip over him, landing behind him and pulling her own dagger from her side, tapping him on the shoulder with the point.

"That would not be a fatal blow," was all he said as he glanced back to the knife.

Before Willow could respond, he spun around, grabbing her wrist and twisting so that she dropped the knife.

"Fuck," Willow muttered as he let go and she went to rub her wrist, though she didn't seem to be in pain.

Her father gave her an apologetic look. "Don't give your enemies the chance to turn on you, *Irathen*. Be more direct with your strikes. You could have killed me before I had even realised you were striking."

Willow looked away. "I don't want to permanently hurt anyone."

His apologetic look turned to a reassuring smile as he took her hands in his. "You don't have to, *Irathen*. This is just training, you aren't hurting me. And you never have to hurt anyone in the future. You don't have to walk my path, and I would never want you to if you weren't sure that it was what you wanted. At your age, I didn't want to either."

"What changed your mind?"

"I saw first-hand what corrupt leaders can do when my father died." He sighed. "I hope that you never see anything that changes your mind."

"If you're hoping that I don't change my mind, why are you training me?"

"I may hope that you don't change your mind, *Irathen*, but that doesn't mean that I think that it's likely. A life caught between two worlds can be a difficult one if corrupt leaders choose to make it so. And they will always choose to make it so."

Willow folded her arms and looked away, her gaze falling on me.

Her pensive look turned to a smile and it took me a moment to figure out why.

She and her father had been so involved in their battle, I'd assumed that they couldn't see me.

But Willow bounded over to me with a grin. "Amelia! What are you doing here?"

I didn't know how to answer that.

I couldn't see any indication that she knew that this was all in her mind, and I wasn't sure how she would react if I told her.

But, before I could worry too much about responding, Willow placed her hand on my cheek, drawing me close before capturing my lips with hers.

I melted into her, unable to focus on anything but the feel of her lips against mine as I realised that some part of me – a not insignificant part – had feared that I would never feel it again.

I kept my hands on her waist as she pulled away, refusing to let her go too far.

"I'm so glad you're here," Willow said. "I've missed you."

"I've missed you too," I said, barely managing to get the words out past my realisation of how true they were.

I wondered if Willow knew.

Something about her bittersweet, longing look told me that she did.

Told me that some part of her understood her predicament.

And had feared, just as much as I had, that she would never wake up.

A throat cleared and I turned, my face heating, to see Willow's father approaching.

He turned to his daughter. "I take it this is your *Ni'tal*?"

Willow turned as red as I was sure I was before turning to me, something hot and fierce in her gaze. "Yes, she is."

Her father smiled, though it was short-lived as he turned to me. "You're not supposed to be here, are you?"

My heart stopped for a moment, as I thought that he was expressing disapproval of me.

Saying that I wasn't good enough for his daughter.

But no, this wasn't really Willow's father.

And I wasn't supposed to be there.

I was intruding in her mind, and while I had good reason, I was still an intruder.

And whatever part of her mind her father represented knew that.

Maybe it was the part that understood Willow's current predicament.

"I'm here to help Willow wake up," I decided to say, deciding to take the chance and hope that he knew what I meant. "I was hoping that you might know more about what's affecting her."

He nodded. "Of course. The fog."

Willow gripped my hands tight at that. "No, Amelia. You can't go there. It's too dangerous. We're staying away, and it's stopped spreading, but if you get too close..."

I gave her a reassuring smile, bringing one of my hands to her cheek.

She leaned into the reassuring touch.

"I promise, I won't get close. I just need to see it for myself."

Willow didn't look happy at that, but she didn't argue.

Her father turned to me. "Come on, I can lead you to it."

I nodded, taking Willow's hand once more as I wondered if she would come with me, or if whatever this fog was scared her too much.

But she squeezed my hand instead of letting it go, and then followed her father, leading me down to the other end of the field.

As we made our way to the edge, I frowned.

I thought it had just been heat haze obscuring my vision in the distance. Or maybe the limits of Willow's dream.

But no, as I approached the edge of the field, I realised that the ground was disintegrating, the particles drifting up into the air, but then just hanging there, lazily floating up and down.

I focused back down at the ground and realised that while it was part-way through disintegrating, the pace was incredibly slow, the particles breaking apart so slowly, I had to watch for a minute or two to even be sure that they were still moving.

"It's draining her lifeforce," I said with a sigh. "I already knew that."

Willow's father nodded. "Unfortunately, that's all we know. Whatever is draining it is too weak to get a read on. And it's not draining very efficiently. It's enough to keep us unconscious, but that's it. Just a slow trickle away, slightly faster than we can replenish it. If the intent were to keep us asleep, there are easier ways to do it. And if the intent were to kill us, this isn't going to manage it. No, whatever this was meant to be, it's a failure."

"Unless the intent was to knock out a large number of people and leave us scrambling as to how to wake you."

"Well, yes, I suppose. You think this was an attack against the school?"

I sighed. "I'm not sure what else it could be. And it's awfully convenient that it happened just as the Slayers arrived."

"Well, if it is their doing, they've covered their tracks well. The lifeforce isn't being directed anywhere, so there's no source to the spell.

No evidence to find. And it's not strong enough to sense the kind of magic that originated it. Short of a confession, I do not think you'll find your culprit."

"Which means that I won't be able to rely on them lifting the spell."

"Indeed."

Willow squeezed my hand once more, drawing my attention to her. "If anyone can figure it out, it's you."

I tried to return the smile she was giving me, but it was hard when I wasn't sure that I'd earned her faith in me.

"I love you," I said, the words blurting out of my mouth as I realised that I wasn't sure that I would be able to wake her.

That I would ever see her again.

That I might have squandered my one chance to say it to her properly.

Before Willow could respond, I was back in my chair in the infirmary, tears streaming down my cheeks.

I went to wipe them with the back of my sleeve.

"Here."

I almost jumped out of my chair as I realised that Mr Stiles was standing beside me, handing me a tissue.

"Thanks," I said.

"So, what did Willow have to say?" he asked. "I'm assuming that you sneaked in here to try to form some kind of connection with her. Was she aware?"

"Not exactly. It was like a dream... But some part of her knew what was happening and told me that her lifeforce is being drained."

Mr Stiles sighed. "We'd already managed to piece that much together. Was there anything else? Maybe where the lifeforce was being directed?"

"It wasn't really being directed anywhere. It was just kind of swirling around once it was taken from her."

Mr Stiles frowned. "That's not good. I mean, it's good that no one's feeding on her, but if her lifeforce isn't being directed anywhere, we can't follow it to the source."

"Yeah, that's what she said. Kind of. I think it was her. Or part of her. And she said that she couldn't sense who was behind it either. The spell causing it is too weak."

"Which means that we're back to square one."

I cringed. "Is there really nothing else we can do? Some way to track down the source of the spell?"

"We're still not even sure that it is a spell. Like you said, if there is a spell, it's too weak to sense. It might still be some kind of illness. But if that's the case, then we don't understand how it's being transmitted. Or where it came from." He sighed before giving me a reassuring smile. "But don't worry, we're working on it. This was a good idea, but your focus should be on your studies. Now, get going, or you'll be late for your first class."

I COULDN'T FOCUS THROUGH my morning lessons.

Both because I was worried for Willow, and also because in my haste to get to the infirmary, I'd forgotten to take my ADHD medication.

Or brush my teeth, or get breakfast...

I tried to make-do with strong coffee, but it barely helped.

I managed to get back to my room at break to brush my teeth, but I was too close to my lunchtime tablet to take my morning one, so my focus didn't return until lunch.

Marking another lost day of A-Level studies.

And another day that I just didn't care.

Not with everything else going on.

Though, I sighed as I realised that my next class was Non-Spellcraft Magic, and that my new-found focus was probably wasted there.

After all, without Willow to teach me, what was the point?

Natalie gave me a sympathetic look as soon as we approached the classroom, presumably realising the same thing I just had.

"We'll talk to Miss Tilly," she said. "She'll know how to help."

I nodded, though I wasn't so sure.

Or maybe the reminder that Willow was still unconscious had put me in too much of a melancholy to care.

Tears threatened to well in my eyes as I remembered finally telling her that I loved her, right as I left her mind.

Would she even remember my visit?

Was she aware of it?

Or did it not even matter?

Had I lost my chance to tell her for real the moment her lifeforce had started draining?

I was barely aware of Natalie leading me to the front of the classroom, where Miss Tilly was standing, until I recognised that Miss Tilly was giving me the same sympathetic look everyone else had been.

My stomach twisted with agitation at that. Why was everyone looking at me like that?

I didn't want their pity. I didn't ask for it.

But I took a deep breath, remembering a YouTube video I'd watched on ADHD and stress.

And how emotional dysregulation can lead to picking fights.

Like the fight with the Slayer.

But that asshole had been asking for it.

Miss Tilly and Natalie weren't.

But letting go of the anger was hard.

Not least because I could feel the tears welling beneath it and raging in the classroom would at least leave me feeling in control.

Bursting into tears would leave me a mess.

Miss Tilly looked me over before turning to Natalie. "Would you mind looking after the class for today, Natalie? I think Amelia could use some quiet tutoring."

Natalie nodded. "Of course."

"Come on," Miss Tilly said to me. "Next door should be empty."

I just nodded, following her out of the classroom.

I had no idea what she intended, but I was afraid of what might come out of my mouth if I tried to ask.

Miss Tilly took me to the empty classroom next door before closing the door and casting a privacy spell before turning to me.

"How are you holding up with Willow in the infirmary?"

I folded my arms. "I'm fine," I managed, not sure what else to say.

"No, you're not. You've been through a lot in the last couple of months, Amelia. Being attacked by Demons, your mum being cursed, realising you're a Witch, coming into your magic, being tricked by Maria, having to go through the Amazons' trials... And Willow's your first love, isn't she?"

I just nodded, again, not trusting myself to speak.

"Magical beings experience emotions more intensely than Humans. Love can tear us apart if we let it. Or it can fuel us. Drive us forward. How we utilise it will depend on how our magic works, however. Tell me, is there any part of magic that draws you in?"

I nodded, a little relieved as I realised this wasn't just a heart-to-heart.

It was the lesson.

"I... I actually have an easier time with magic tied to Nature."

Miss Tilly raised an eyebrow. "Well, I was thinking more in terms of Light and Dark. But that is still something... You are aware that being in-tune with Nature is unusual for a Witch, yes?"

I shrugged. "I know, but there's some magic, like healing magic, that I can only do if I use techniques developed by elemental beings."

Miss Tilly nodded. "The healing magic Witches usually use is based in Light magic. Tell me, how do you fare with other uses of Light magic?"

"I... When I stopped Maria Brown's spell on Samhain, I used Light magic to do it."

"And have you used it since?"

I looked away.

"Light and Dark don't usually run in families for Witches. Some pretend that they do, but it truly is individual. But you're not just a Witch, are you? No, there's clearly another connection there. Tell me, do you have any Demons in your family?"

I still didn't meet her gaze, unsure of what to say. Mentioning my connection to Freya could be deadly, and I wasn't sure if I trusted her yet.

But she gave me a reassuring smile. "Ah, of course. You need not worry, Amelia. The Fae still retain knowledge that many have forgotten, so I realised you were Angelborn some time ago. I had no idea if you even knew of the term, however, and I didn't want to draw attention to something that might cause you trouble in the long run. But if you already know, then you must also know that the only Angel of Life alive to create you was Queen Freya, and she's half-Demon."

I just stood there, unsure of what to say. She'd clearly figured it all out, so denying it seemed pointless, but...

"Don't worry," she said, "I have no intention of telling anyone. Which is why I never mentioned it before. Given the rarity of Angels, it's probably a good thing that Angelborn have faded from memory. Does anyone else know? I assume your aunt does."

"She, Ms Griffin, Mr Stiles and Sarah all know."

"Gail makes sense as the head of the school, and everyone knows that Sarah used to be friends with Freya, but Aaron?" She cocked her head to the side. "I suppose Freya sent him here, then? So, she knows of your existence? I had wondered, given her age when you would have been conceived. I honestly wouldn't have thought she was powerful enough to create an Angelborn at that age, never mind do it consciously. Though I suppose that would have been around the time of the magical excess in the city, so maybe she tapped into that..."

I folded my arms with a frown. "You're talking like you know her."

"We met briefly. My brother isn't as friendly as I am, and he... Well, he was trying to save her, but Peter's never been one to think things through. To be honest, I'm surprised that he never visited you, but then, Freya might have killed him for that."

None of that really made any sense to me, but Miss Tilly was shaking her head before I could ask.

"Regardless, I just wanted to know who knew so that I wasn't watching what I said around people who already knew the truth. But I have no interest in telling anyone else. I know that you're still new to magic and still trying to figure yourself out, and I would never want to make that harder for you. But that does beg the question, does your connection to Freya leave you more in-tune with Dark magic than Light? You're no Demon, but you carry her magic within you, and that might cause you to lean more towards Dark magic than Light."

I tightened my arms over my chest. "I... I'm not sure. You know, when I first came here, I kind of hoped that I would be a Dark Witch so that I could go to the Underworld to see Freya again. But now?" I sighed. "I just don't understand why I have to choose. I mean, I've drawn from both kinds of magic, so even if I do prefer one over the other, why would I restrict myself?"

"You don't have to choose, Amelia. But if you do have an easier time with Dark Energy than Light, it would make sense for you to acknowledge that and focus on magics that need Dark Energy, rather than trying to struggle with Light."

I sighed before biting my lip as I thought over her point.

"My auntie isn't Light or Dark, is she?" I eventually asked.

"No. And to my knowledge, neither is Maria Brown."

My blood ran cold. "Ma- Maria Brown? Why... Why would you bring her up?"

Miss Tilly once again gave me a reassuring smile. "She was tutoring you, wasn't she? Before she revealed who she truly was, I mean."

"Right. But then she revealed who she truly was..."

She nodded. "So, you think I was making the comparison as a negative one?" She shook her head. "No, I know how to read people well enough to know what was a facade with Maria and what wasn't. I thought she had something a little less dramatic to hide, but I know what was her attempting to hide things and what was her being genuine. And I quite liked her. She was troubled, definitely, but I did not believe that it was to such an extent that distance was required."

"How do you know when distance is required?"

"Experience." She shrugged. "You get burned enough, you learn when someone is beyond help. Or, at least, beyond your help. Maria didn't strike me as someone who had reached that point. She seemed lost, and maybe too stuck in her own head to see the forest for the trees, but not beyond help. So, I didn't bring her up as a negative comparison. Just one that might make sense to you."

I nodded, still not entirely sure how to take that. So, I opted for changing the subject. "Willow was helping me with Nature magic. Could you do the same? I don't know much about Fae magic, but you said yours was elemental..."

"Some Fae, like me, are connected to Nature. We're all born from Angels, or other Fae, so it's simply a matter of tracing our lineage. My mother was descended from Nature, so I'm tied to her. I can help you with your study of Nature magic today, as there was no Slayer in the class. But when they're watching, we won't be able to leave the class, and I doubt you want them realising that you're anything more than an ordinary Witch."

"Yeah, no. Best that they stay in the dark. But... Could you teach me healing magic? Willow taught me an Elven technique, and it's the only time I've ever been able to heal. If I can get stronger, maybe I can help Willow."

Miss Tilly then gave me a sympathetic look. "Amelia... If Sarah is struggling this much to heal them, then they are likely beyond conventional healing. Even healing that is tied to Nature. You would need something much stronger."

I sighed, remembering the story we'd come across in the library, of a Daughter of Nature petitioning her mother to help her heal a village. "If only we had an Angel..."

I then frowned, turning to Miss Tilly. "Wait, if your mother was tied to Nature, could you petition Nature to help us? I came across a tale in the library of a Daughter asking Nature to help her heal a village."

Miss Tilly shook her head. "My grandmother was the Daughter of Nature, and I think it was a shock to everyone when my brother and I showed more affinity for Nature than Life, given that our mother's Angel of Life nature almost completely obscured that part of her heritage. But even with that affinity, Nature has never answered me, or any other Fae."

I tried not to look too disappointed. It wasn't her fault Nature had never answered her.

Miss Tilly continued, however. "Though, while Nature may have never spoken to me, that doesn't mean that she won't speak to you."

"I'm not a Daughter of Nature either."

"No, but you're not Fae. She might answer you where she doesn't answer me."

"So... how would I call to her?"

Miss Tilly smiled. "Here, I'll show you. You'll have to wait until the end of the day to get somewhere closer to her domain, but I can at least explain what to do when you get there."

AFTER MY LAST LESSON ended, I headed straight for the woods outside the school.

And the spot where I found my wand.

The spot close to Nature.

Only, as I rounded the corner from my last class, I almost ran right into Mr Stiles, barely stopping myself in time.

"Amelia," he said as he saw me. "Ready for some more training?"

"Actually, I can't today. When reading up on how to help Willow and the others, I found a story about a Daughter of Nature asking her mother to help her heal a village. I figured that I could do the same."

Mr Stiles frowned for a moment before sighing. "Right, because of..." He waved his hand and I got the sense that he was avoiding saying 'Freya' where a Slayer might hear him. "She might not answer you. You're not one of her Daughters."

"I know, but it's worth a try."

He frowned once more.

"Unless you think it's not?"

"Come on," he said. "Let's head outside. I'm assuming you have a spot in mind?"

I nodded, and headed outside, while Mr Stiles followed.

Once we were outside, he cast a privacy spell, though he didn't say anything.

"Do you have a problem with this plan?" I asked again, hoping that he would answer now that we were away from prying ears.

He sighed. "I just... I've never met Nature, but her Daughters can either be closer to her or closer to humanity. Freya used to be closer to humanity, but then she almost died, and she was only able to survive by shedding her humanity and becoming closer to Nature. It changed her."

"In a bad way?"

He sighed once more, clearly buying time to get his thoughts into place before answering.

"It wasn't bad or good," he eventually said. "It was just different. But if Nature is even more removed than Freya became, she might not want to help. She might not care."

I frowned. "How could she not care? People are being hurt."

"*People* aren't Nature's domain. That's why she has her Daughters. To bridge the gap."

"Well, I might not be one of her Daughters, but we are connected. If they can make her care, so can I."

Mr Stiles didn't argue with me as we made our way into the woods, so I just led him to the clearing where I'd found my wand.

Though as we approached, it wasn't finding my wand that I remembered.

No, it was coming here with Willow.

Sitting beside her as we talked for hours, our hands entwined as we slowly got closer and closer...

My heart panged at the memory, but I steeled myself.

Standing here and panicking about Willow wouldn't save her.

But Nature might.

I turned to Mr Stiles. "I'm going to try to call to Nature."

He nodded. "I'll wait outside the clearing for you. She might not show if I'm here, but I'll be close if you need me."

"Okay," I said, not exactly happy with the thought of being left alone but knowing that he was right.

Mr Stiles turned and left the clearing, and I had to admit that I felt better once I was alone.

As if there was something about the clearing that couldn't fully manifest as long as Mr Stiles was there.

But now that he was gone, it was as if the colours were turned up to eleven.

I kneeled in the grass, before the largest tree, just as Miss Tilly had told me to.

I reached out with my magic, sensing the life around me.

The same life that I drew on for the healing spell that Willow taught me.

I didn't draw from it, but I could sense it.

And I could sense that it knew that I was there.

"Nature," I called. "I am asking for your aid. Please hear me."

Miss Tilly hadn't said that it was necessary to say anything – she'd said that Nature would know that I was calling to her as soon as I entered the clearing with intent, and all I had to do was show that I was humbly asking for her help – but I figured that speaking aloud would probably help.

I waited on my knees as the damp of the ground soaked into my trousers, and I shivered slightly.

I had no idea how long I had been kneeling there when I heard a knock on one of the trees behind me.

I hurriedly spun around, expecting to see Nature.

But no.

Mr Stiles was standing by the edge of the clearing, his fist raised to one of the trees in a knocking motion.

"Anything?" he asked.

I sighed. "No. Nothing."

He gave me a sympathetic look. "Maybe that's for the best. As I said, we have no idea what would have happened if Nature actually had showed up."

I nodded, though I didn't exactly buy that logic.

How could she possibly make things worse from here?

"Come on," Mr Stiles said. "Let's get back to training."

"Yeah," I said, figuring that I had more than enough fuel for Dark Energy.

I TRUDGED UP TO MY and Natalie's room thoroughly exhausted by my training.

And still feeling like shit, despite trying to fuel all my frustration into Dark Energy during my training.

But now I still felt awful, and I was tired.

Great...

Natalie looked up from her laptop as I entered the room, immediately setting it down next to her on her bed. "You okay?"

I sighed. "No." I flopped down onto my bed, not caring if I sounded pathetic.

I wasn't in the mood to pretend that I was okay just to make other people comfortable.

"Still worried about Willow?"

"Of course."

Natalie made her way over at that, sitting down next to me before almost placing her hand on my shoulder, though it just hovered there instead of giving me a comforting touch.

I sighed, sitting up and drawing my knees to my chest, hugging them tight. "I thought maybe I could ask Nature for help, like that story we found in the library. I know that I'm not one of her Daughters, but I am connected to her through Freya, so I thought..."

Natalie nodded, placing her hands in her lap. Evidently giving up on attempting any kind of physical comfort. "You thought that Nature would help you?"

"Yep. But she didn't even answer me, Natalie. Maybe I did something wrong, but... Maybe I just don't have enough of a connection."

"Maybe... But like you said, maybe you made a mistake. We could go and ask Lena. I mean, she's an elemental being, so maybe she can help."

I bit my lip.

"Unless you don't want to?"

"No, I do. I mean, I want this to work! But..."

Natalie gave me one of her soft, understated smiles, and I knew that she understood. "You don't want to get your hopes up again."

I sighed. "Yeah. But that's not a reason not to try, is it? So, you're right. I should talk to Lena."

Natalie smiled as she stood up before offering her hand.

I took it, stumbling to my feet before following her out of the door and towards Lena and Charlotte's room.

Natalie knocked on the door before just letting herself in, getting past the wards to the room just like the others can do for our room.

"Hey-" Natalie started, but stopped dead immediately.

I frowned, peering past her only to see Charlotte lying awkwardly on the floor, out cold, while Lena fretted next to her.

"Nat, Lia, thank the Creator," Lena said as soon as she saw us, tears welling in her eyes. "We were just talking, and then she said that she felt faint and..."

She turned back to Charlotte and I got the impression that she was struggling to keep her tears from falling.

Nat hurried over to her and I followed now that the way was clear, both of us kneeling next to her.

"We can shift her to the infirmary," I said. "She'll be okay."

"This is just like what happened to the others, isn't it? You say that she'll be okay, but..."

"But we'll wake her up with everyone else. I promise." I somehow managed to get the words out with far more confidence than I felt, and Lena, thankfully, nodded.

I wasn't sure if she believed that Charlotte would be okay, but she at least knew that she needed help.

I turned to Natalie and she placed her hand on Lena's shoulder as I placed mine on Charlotte's, before we shifted them to the infirmary.

We arrived in what was possibly the only empty spot in the room, beds crammed in every other space.

All filled with unconscious students.

I stared around the room, losing count as I tried to figure out how many students there were.

Too many, was the only answer I could come up with.

Sarah rushed over as soon as she saw us. "Charlotte?"

I nodded.

She shook her head. "Give me a moment to get another bed."

I nodded again as Sarah headed off.

I turned back to Lena, seeing that she hadn't let go of Charlotte's hand.

"Are you okay?" I asked.

"No," she said. "How can I be? No one knows how to wake any of them up. And no one seems to have any leads on how to figure it out."

"That's not true. When we came to your room-"

Before I could finish, the door to the infirmary slammed open, and we all turned to see Michael storming into the room.

He narrowed his eyes as he finally spotted Sarah. "This is getting ridiculous," he bellowed at her.

She refused to answer, her back to him.

I had no idea if she actually didn't know that he was there – I didn't know how her captioning glasses actually worked, and I guessed it made sense that they had limitations – or if she was just pretending not to know to annoy him, but the effect was the same.

Michael stood there, clearly fuming, before moving to loom over her shoulder, waiting for her to turn around from the student she was examining.

She didn't turn, however. Instead, she said, "You're in my light."

Michael looked like he was about to burst a blood vessel, and I was sure that he was going to grab Sarah and forcibly move her.

But then Sarah did turn, glaring at him. "You're still in my light. I know that you Slayers have little love for Healers, but I am still an Amazon."

That seemed to be enough to get him to finally back down, even if it took a moment of him returning her glare before he finally stepped back.

"You're right, I apologise, but I don't think you're treating this situation with the gravity it deserves. This clearly isn't an illness. Only a curse acts like this."

"Why are you telling me?"

"Because that damn deputy headteacher is road blocking me. She won't give me any information on Maria Brown's time at the school."

"Maria Brown has been gone for weeks."

"And she could have left a curse behind. But the deputy isn't taking this seriously. She won't give me the information I need."

"So, you want me to get it?"

"No. I'm warning you that I'm going to get it by any means necessary." He growled his words as lightning crackled over his arms.

He glared at Sarah, and I shivered as I realised that he wasn't messing around.

That he was determined to pin this on Maria.

A dead-end route, but one that would surely lead to me.

And stop me from being able to actually help.

I didn't breathe again until he finally turned and left the room.

Once the door closed behind him, I spun back to Lena.

"Lena, I tried to call to Nature to ask her to help heal everyone, but she didn't respond. I was wondering if I might have been doing something wrong."

Lena didn't answer me for a moment, and I wasn't sure that she'd even heard me, all of her attention on Charlotte.

But, eventually, she said, "When did you do this?"

"After last lesson."

"So, what? An hour ago?"

"Yeah."

She shook her head, still not looking up to face me. "Lia, people spend days wandering the wilderness, hoping that Nature will answer them. You have to give it more than an hour."

I bit my lip, very glad that I hadn't admitted that it had really been more like ten minutes.

"Thank you," I said as Sarah returned to help get Charlotte onto a bed.

Lena didn't respond.

I considered staying with her, but Natalie put her hand on my shoulder.

"What are you planning?" she asked.

I sighed. "Someone needs to stay here with Lena."

"I don't think Sarah's going to let her stay. Not when it's so crowded. But I can make sure she's okay."

"Then I think I have to go back to the clearing."

"For how long? You can't go further into the woods, the warding spells around the school won't let you. Especially not now we're in quarantine. And Lena said it could take days."

"I don't think I can skip classes tomorrow without anyone noticing. And if the Slayers notice, it probably won't take them long to discover how involved I was with everything that went on with Maria. But I can stay the night, at least."

Natalie frowned. "In the woods? Alone?"

"I'll be fine. I'll take a blanket."

"And what if Nature doesn't answer you? Or what if she does, but she doesn't appreciate your intrusion?"

"I don't know, but I have to try."

She regarded me carefully for a moment before nodding with a small sigh. "Of course, you do. Just... Be careful?"

"I will. I promise."

Chapter Nine

I returned to the woods that night, taking a blanket with me to ward off the chill of the night air, though I wrapped it around my shoulders, still kneeling in the damp grass, despite the chill.

I needed Nature to know that I was there.

That I was calling to her.

Though as the hours waned, I doubted more and more that I would ever get a response.

I leaned back against one of the larger trees, the busy day taking its toll as the last remnants of any ADHD medication in my system left, and I had to fight against my exhaustion, not wanting to fall asleep and potentially miss Nature appearing.

But as I struggled to keep my eyes open, I was sure that I lost a few hours to sleep.

Though it wasn't restful enough for me to see Maria.

Eventually, as the first trickles of dawn's light started to filter through the trees, I jumped at the sound of rustling branches.

I leapt to my feet, worried that one of the Slayers had found me, hunting for Maria's accomplice.

But as I looked to the sound, I instead found myself staring into a pair of startlingly green eyes, surrounded by shaggy white fur.

A wolf.

I was staring at a wolf.

The wolf turned and bounded off and it took me a moment to realise that there shouldn't be any wolves here.

I scrambled after it, leaving my blanket behind as I headed deeper into the woods.

"Wait!" I called, but the wolf didn't stop.

No, it just turned a corner and disappeared into the trees.

I ran after it, only for the trees to open up, almost blinding sunlight hitting my eyes.

I raised my hand to cover my face, taking a moment for my eyesight to adjust.

But when it did, I realised that I was in another clearing, this one brighter than the last, with every colour seeming highly saturated as a rainbow of flowers grew in soft green grass, surrounding a bright blue pond, which was being filled from a small waterfall down the rocks that made up the other side of the clearing.

I definitely wasn't at school anymore...

"Well, aren't you a surprise."

I spun around at the stranger's voice, that somehow sounded like a soft breeze through rain, to see a tall woman with the same startling green eyes as the wolf, and skin that seemed to be made of bark.

Water ran from her head like hair, trickling down to embers in her wooden skin and making sure that they remained embers whenever they flared up and threatened to consume her.

So, this was Nature.

There was no other conclusion I could come to. None of the books I'd read about her had been consistent in their descriptions, but I recognised enough.

I briefly wondered if that was because the records were kept poorly, or if she changed how her form looked over time, but then she was speaking again.

"You're not one of my Daughters, are you? And yet, you're also not a normal Witch. How fascinating... Perhaps I have been approaching this all wrong."

I frowned. "All what wrong?"

"My Daughters no longer bridge the gap between myself and humanity, as they are supposed to. How could they, with things so out of balance? I have taken a different approach – a painful approach – with my youngest. But you? You might be able to act as a bridge without the danger my Daughters face."

"Danger?"

The water flowed more heavily from Nature's head. "In order to use their powers, my Daughters must become more like me. They must be as in tune with Nature as they are with Humanity. But we are burning," the embers flared up to flames, sending a hiss of steam into the air, "and my Daughters cannot handle the strain.

"Freya hides from the pain in the Underworld, and my youngest... I hope that I have kept her safe, but the closer she gets to uncovering her powers, the more I worry that it isn't enough."

The flames died down as she cocked her head. "But you did not come here to be my bridge, did you? Tell me, child, why did you call me?"

"There's some kind of magical sickness or curse affecting the school, and none of us know how to stop it. I read in one of the books in the library that one of your Daughters once asked you to heal a village afflicted with a sickness that no one else could cure."

"Ah, yes. Amaka. Unfortunately, your tale does not tell the story true. I did not heal the village for Amaka. The closer to me my Daughters are, the more power they have. Amaka shed her humanity to gain the strength she needed. She saved the village, but she was not the same woman as before. Not that that is necessarily a bad thing, but if you want that kind of power, you would have to do the same."

A chill went through me at the thought of changing myself so fundamentally.

Of losing part of what made me Human.

But, well, I wasn't Human, was I?

I was a Witch. An Angelborn.

"I'll do it," I said, no hint of doubt in my voice. "I'll shed my humanity if it will save Willow and Charlotte and the others."

"You speak of Willow with love. If you do this, you may not be able to return to her. You will no longer be the girl she fell in love with."

"That doesn't matter. As long as she's alive and well, that doesn't matter."

Nature gave me a bittersweet smile. "Freya once said something very similar. And I am afraid that her choice almost killed her."

"If that's the price for everyone else's lives, then it's worth it."

"That's also what she said." Nature then looked down at my arm and I realised that she was looking at where I had rolled my sleeves up, my scars visible beneath.

"You've already been down this path before," Nature noted. "Would you repeat the past?"

"That was different. I didn't understand what I was doing then."

"And you understand now?"

I frowned, not seeing what she was getting at.

"I cannot heal the school for you, and I am not sure that you could shed your humanity to gain the powers of a Daughter if you tried. But perhaps I can help you see clearly."

"How?"

"By changing you. Not as much as shedding your humanity would, but there will be a change."

"What kind of change?"

"I can awaken the part of my magic that you carry within you. As I said, I don't think that it will give you the power of a Daughter, you are still a Witch, after all. But it will make you something else. Not a Witch and not a Daughter. Something without a home."

"I'm already that. I've been that for as long as I can remember."

"Then drink."

Nature gestured to the pool beside her and I hesitated.

"From the pool?"

She nodded and I steeled myself, my surety failing as I was faced with the reality of actually going through with this.

But I had to.

There was no other choice.

I made my way over to the pool and kneeled, cupping my hands to pick up some of the water.

I brought it to my lips, and I suddenly felt as if I hadn't drunk in days, draining my hands dry in seconds.

I almost went for a second drink, but I was pulled back by Nature's hand on my shoulder.

"It looks like that part of your magic has just been waiting for you to awaken it. But let's not overdo it. How do you feel?"

"I..."

I struggled to get words out as the world started to hum around me, buzzing with life.

It was like another sense that I couldn't control or shut off, overwhelming everything else.

And Nature?

She was like a beacon beside me, blinding me.

"I can feel everything," I eventually managed. "Every butterfly, every blade of grass... It's like they're singing over the top of each other, while flashing different coloured strobe lights."

"Amplifying your connection to me has meant amplifying your connection to every living creature. And that connection will bring you insight. Insight that may help solve your current crisis."

"I... Thank you," I managed as I finally managed to think past the distracting noise.

The noise was still there, but the less novel it became, the easier it was to ignore.

Nature smiled. "It was a pleasure. You may not be one of my Daughters, but you are close enough to ease the pain of being separated from them."

"You're really avoiding your youngest?"

"I believe that it is the best way to keep her safe."

I nodded. "Well, I could call to you again. Not to ask for help, but just to talk. You know, if you want."

"I think I would like that. But for now, go. Your friends need you."

I HAD A SPLITTING HEADACHE as I returned to the school, the noise of the life around me still causing some discomfort.

And even if that discomfort was easing, I was still exhausted from awakening that part of my powers.

But as I left the woods and approached the school, the noise changed.

It was no longer a steady hum, every part working in tandem to create a somewhat coherent whole.

No, now everything was screaming.

I frowned, looking at the air as the noise turned to coloured streaks of light.

Life force.

Only it wasn't staying in place.

No, as I ventured back to the school and started to see other students heading to breakfast, I realised that it was being pulled from everyone.

A strand here, a strand there.

The ones in the infirmary were just unlucky enough to have had too much taken.

I looked down at myself and gave a sigh of relief.

My life force wasn't going anywhere.

Evidence that Maria's protection spell had worked.

I promised myself that I would thank her the next time I saw her before turning my attention back to the life force around me, and its random swirling in the air.

Or... It was random, wasn't it?

I frowned as I watched.

It looked random.

It looked like it didn't have a purpose.

But... No.

The more I watched, the more I saw the pattern, slow and lazy, but eerily familiar.

"Shit," I muttered before following the pattern back to the infirmary.

I headed inside, ignoring the unconscious students as I approached the dead spot in the energy.

The eye of the storm.

The one person in the school, other than me, whose lifeforce wasn't being drawn into the air.

"Amelia," Mr Stiles said as I approached, a deep frown forming as I got close. "What happened to your eye?"

I ignored the question, my mind unable to process it as I realised what was happening.

And that I had no idea how to say it.

We hadn't released Maria's spell properly.

We'd released it from Mr Stiles, but it hadn't dissipated.

And without another host to draw from, it was taking what it could from anyone nearby.

I looked away, unable to meet his gaze, only for my eyes to fall on two unconscious forms.

Natalie and Lena.

Mr Stiles gave me a sympathetic look as he realised where my gaze had gone.

"Lena got woozy before she left, and Natalie stayed to help, only for her to pass out as well."

"How many students are still conscious?"

He sighed. "Honestly? We're not sure. Not until we check who's unconscious in their rooms. But not many."

Before I could formulate another thought, the door to the infirmary slammed open.

"I don't care if Gail made you her deputy, you are obviously covering for Maria Brown's accomplice. I know that she had help from a student and your railroading might be costing these students their lives."

I turned at the sound of Michael's voice to see him and my auntie entering the room.

Auntie Jess was glaring at him. "We don't know that this had anything to do with Maria-"

"Of course, we do. Who else could it be? And when I find her accomplice, I will make sure she pays for the lives she has taken here."

"No one is dead yet and you cannot blame a student for trusting someone who lied to her."

"I can and will. Someone has to pay for what has happened here. Or *will* happen here, but your faith that these students will awaken is naive."

At that, Michael waved his hand across the room, his gaze finally meeting my own.

As soon as he saw me, he glared, electricity sparking up his arms.

"What the- *Of course*. Of course, it would be your niece. Of course, you would try to protect her."

"Michael, you have no idea what might have caused this. There's no reason to think that it might have been Maria-"

"Then what other explanation do you have?"

I frowned as he turned back to me with narrowed eyes.

What the hell was he seeing that caused this suspicion?

"Explanation for what?" I demanded, my patience destroyed by seeing both Lena and Natalie unconscious.

And realising that Michael wasn't wrong to be suspicious of me.

If I hadn't helped Maria, none of this would have happened.

And maybe I'd been the one to screw up Sarah's spell to free Mr Stiles. Maybe if I'd let her do it alone...

Auntie Jess looked me over with a concerned frown. "You mean you don't know?"

"Don't know what?"

"Your eye..."

Michael turned to her before she could explain further. "You've been protecting her for too long, Jessica. I've been wracking my brain, wondering why you would be protecting Maria's accomplice. Why you would be hiding her from justice. And now your niece, who you swore to me was nothing more than an unusually powerful Witch, is showing signs of being a Daughter of Nature. If you lied about this, why wouldn't you have been lying about her being Maria's accomplice?"

"That's a stretch and you know it."

"You know what's not a stretch? The fact that she's one of the only students yet to succumb to this curse. It would make sense that Maria would protect her protégé."

"I'm not a Daughter of Nature," I eventually managed, knowing that I had no defence when it came to Maria.

I had been her accomplice, after all.

And she was protecting me from the spell.

But I didn't think Michael had any intention of using that fact to help break the spell.

No, he wasn't looking to cure anyone.

He was out for vengeance.

I will make sure she pays for the lives she has taken here, he'd said when demanding that my auntie turn me over.

He'd already written off the students here. They weren't lives to save, they were crimes to pin me with.

"I just went to Nature to ask for her help," I continued. "She helped me to see what was happening."

Michael's glare didn't let up. "Nature doesn't respond to just anyone's call. You don't have elemental blood and you're not one of her Daughters. Why would she answer you?"

"I don't care if you believe that she was the one to help, just that you believe that I know what's causing this and how to stop it."

Michael narrowed his eyes. "A confession?"

I bit my lip.

It wasn't as if he was wrong.

I would have to tell them that Maria's spell had done this.

And I *had* helped her.

But I couldn't risk everyone else in the room to save myself.

I had to tell them the truth.

"The spell Maria Brown cast on Mr Stiles was meant to draw his life force in to power another spell. It was aggressive and difficult to disperse, but Sarah and I managed it. At least, we thought we had." I turned to Mr Stiles. "I'm sorry, but you're the eye of the storm. This spell isn't drawing from you, and the only reason I can think why that might be..."

"Is if you banished the spell from me without dispelling it completely," Mr Stiles said with a sigh.

"Yes. I think it's unstable now, unable to bond to a single host, and so drawing from everyone it can. Not as much as it drew from you, but it doesn't have to be much."

I turned back to Michael to see that he was wearing a coldly smug look.

"So," he said, the smugness permeating his voice as well, "you admit that this was Maria's doing. And for someone others claim wasn't her accomplice, you have an awfully detailed knowledge of her magic. How do I know that you didn't sabotage the dispelling attempt yourself?"

"If I did, would I be here, telling you all of this?"

"Either way, it's clear that you were involved. Which means that I'm taking you into Slayer custody. This is no longer a matter for the school to decide. *I* will be the one who determines your fate."

He stepped towards me, but Auntie Jess moved in front of him, blocking his way.

"Amy is still a student here, and I am still in charge. I did not release her into your custody."

"You do not have a choice," Michael growled. "Gail was chosen to run this school because she was a well-respected Coven Head. But you? You're just a hedge Witch, with no allegiances and no support to call on. Most of your staff is unconscious, whereas most of my Slayers have the fortitude to withstand this spell. You cannot win in a fight against us."

"You underestimate me."

I stepped forward, knowing that Michael was right.

Auntie Jess wouldn't win this fight, and I was afraid of what would happen to her if she tried.

"I'll go with you," I said to Michael.

"Amy-" Auntie Jess started, but I raised my hand to cut her off.

"We need to focus on a way to get rid of this spell for good, not fighting amongst ourselves. If me going with Michael will do that, then it's a small price to pay."

Especially when this really was all my fault.

Everything happening to Willow, to my friends...

"You promised Gail that you would keep the school running," I reminded my auntie. "That has to come first."

I could see the conflict behind her eyes.

She knew that I was right, but she couldn't let me go.

And if I was being honest, if she was the one asking this of me, I'm not sure that I could let her go either.

But I hoped that my auntie had a stronger sense of pragmatism than me.

"All right," Auntie Jess eventually said, before rounding on Michael. "But I swear, if you so much as touch a hair on her head..."

"How Slayers treat their prisoners is no concern of yours, Witch."

At that, Michael marched over to me and grabbed me by the arm, far rougher than he could have possibly thought he needed with a prisoner who was going willingly.

Still, I didn't give him the satisfaction of crying out.

Not least because this was still the right thing, and I didn't want him to succeed in riling up my auntie again.

No, I would endure whatever the Slayers had in store for me.

And trust that Auntie Jess and Mr Stiles could break the spell.

MICHAEL DRAGGED ME through the school, despite the fact that I wasn't resisting him.

Every time I tried to catch up with his pace, he simply moved faster, until I was sure that he was using his magic to speed us through the school.

Which meant that I was going at quite the speed when we reached the Slayer's rooms, and he switched from dragging me to hurling me through one of the doors.

I heard the sickening crack in my ears before I felt the pain, struggling to stand as I slid from the far wall, my shoulder radiating agony from where I'd bounced off it.

I did my best to ignore the pain and take stock of my surroundings.

I was in a room, much like the one I shared with Natalie, but this one only had a bed, and there was no door between the room and the toilet, leaving everything visible.

A cell.

How long ago had the Slayers set this up?

How long had they been planning to find Maria's accomplice and imprison her?

I thanked the Creator that I hadn't actually admitted to helping Maria.

Michael's suspicion was, obviously, correct, but as long as no one else told him that, I was fine.

Though I didn't think that would last long.

I'd passed the Amazons' trials, and they wouldn't incriminate one of their own, but Dana hadn't exactly struck me as the honourable sort.

If Michael went to her and asked for her help, I was pretty sure that she would give it.

Which basically meant that my fate would be decided by whether or not Michael would reach out for help.

I wasn't sure that I liked those odds.

I finally managed to stand somewhat straight, the pain fading, only for my limbs to lock in place as electricity crackled around me.

Michael.

He had his hand outstretched, a wave electricity stemming from it to wrap around me.

He tightened his hand into a fist and the electricity pulled tight, crushing my limbs into my body.

"You will tell me what you did to cause this curse and how to reverse it."

"I didn't do anything," I managed, despite my struggle for air. "I don't know how to reverse it."

The first part was a lie, but I figured the fact that the second wasn't was more important.

Even if I admitted to helping Maria, I had no idea how to fix this.

That's why we were in this mess.

"You can lie all you want, I have ways of making you talk."

The electricity crushed me further as he reached for his sword with his free hand.

I stared at the weapon as I finally realised what he was implying. "You're going to torture me? You can't. I'm a student. And an Amazon. You can't just-"

The electricity let go of me, dropping me to the ground.

I let out a sigh of relief as I finally managed to breathe, but it was short-lived, as Michael grabbed me by my injured arm, pulling me up.

Pain clouded my vision as my arm felt as if it were on fire.

I just needed it to stop.

I needed him to stop.

Why the fuck was he doing this to me???

Dark Energy cascaded from me in a singular blast.

My pain and hurt became physical, knocking away anything that might hurt me.

Keeping me safe.

And destroying my enemies.

I swayed on my feet as the blast cleared, taking a moment to process the destruction of the room around me.

The cracks in the wall, the tattered remains of the bed...

And the Slayer lying bloody and battered against the far wall.

Michael was still conscious, however, glaring at me as he pushed himself to his feet.

"That... That was a Demon technique," he growled, his voice dripping with venom. "You profess your innocence, and yet you use Demon fighting techniques. We suspected that Maria Brown was working with Demons, and now you pretend not to be in league with her, while using their techniques. No, the Demons have always wanted this school for themselves, and they would not be above working with Maria Brown. They were the ones to plant her here, weren't they?"

"What? No! I mean, how should I know?"

Michael didn't answer me, instead leaving the room.

As soon as he was gone, the walls hummed with magic and I gasped, struggling to stay standing as my exhaustion turned from insistent tides to angry waves, not allowing me to swim free.

"What is that?" I managed, my voice frustratingly weak and pathetic.

"Energy draining wards. By the morning, you won't have it in you to fight back."

I managed to stay standing as I glared back at him, but the second he turned his back, I dropped to my knees, unable to hold my weight a moment longer.

I looked over to the remnants of the bed, but the splintered frame looked less than safe, so I simply lay down on the carpet and let my exhaustion take me.

Michael might think I was helpless, but I had one last refuge.

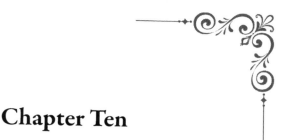

Chapter Ten

I almost cried with relief as I arrived in Maria's lab.

Maria turned to me with a frown. "Amelia! Where have you been? I was so worried when you didn't show up last night. And isn't it mid-morning for you?" She then stopped dead as she got closer. "What happened to your eye?"

I ignored her questions, wrapping my arms tight around her as tears flowed down my cheeks.

Maria tensed for a moment, and I realised what I had done.

I needed someone, but Maria wasn't my mother or my auntie.

Not to mention, she was Litcorde, and if Charlotte was anything to go by, they hated being touched.

But then Maria wrapped her arms around me, her movements still a little stiff but undoubtedly meant to be comforting, and I couldn't bring myself to pull away, the last fragment of my restraint crumbling.

"What happened?" Maria asked, her voice soft.

"I think he's going to kill me," I said, her embrace the only thing giving me enough strength to say the words aloud.

Maria's grip tightened. "Who?"

"Michael. The head of the Slayers. He..."

Maria finally pulled away from me, looking me over with her concerned gaze. "Start at the beginning. Which I suspect is what happened to your eye."

I frowned, wiping my tears away with the end of my sleeve. "Okay, seriously, why do people keep mentioning my eye?"

Maria moved to a small mirror, though she paused before handing it over. "I'm not sure if this will work. I mean, you have been able to interact with the lab more and more..."

"More and more?"

"Remember when you first came here? You weren't corporeal."

"Right. Of course. I'm not really here."

"No, but as the bond has gotten stronger, so too has the magic causing you to manifest here. Or, at least, that's my assumption. I'm not sure if you'll have a reflection, but..."

She handed over the mirror and I took it from her.

My reflection wasn't clear – I seemed almost fuzzy around the edges – but it was unmistakably me.

Except for my right eye, which was no longer the dark brown I was used to.

No, it was a vivid shade of green.

The same green that the wolf's eyes had been.

"I went to ask Nature for help," I eventually said.

"And she answered?"

"Yes. She told me to drink from her pond and it gave me the power to... Well, to see life, I guess. The flow of it around me."

"Nature gave you her blessing?" Maria asked, almost sounding... awed. "I'd heard rumours of elemental beings sometimes receiving it, but a Witch? It's unheard of. But then, so is an Angel of Life also being one of her Daughters, and creating an Angelborn."

She shook her head, her expression sobering. "So, did the gift help? Do you know what's affecting the school?"

I winced, not wanting to say it aloud. "Yes, I do. Mr Stiles... He's a dead-zone. Everyone else's life is being drawn, but not his. And the life... It's trying to form a pattern not unlike the one you used to trap Mr Stiles."

Maria groaned, pinching the bridge of her nose. "Of course. I was so willing to trust that you and Sarah had done this right..."

"Don't blame Sarah. If anyone was likely the one to mess this up, it was me."

"No, it was me," Maria said with a stern look. "Do not blame yourself for this, Amelia. I didn't create this spell to be undone, and I should have focused more on undoing it myself. Sarah is a healer, not a cursebreaker, and you are neither. This is because I failed to clean up my own mess."

"Then help me clean it up now. How do we do this?"

"We can't. You know that I've been looking into this, but I don't have a solution yet. For now, balance must be maintained. The best option would be to go back to the spell draining a singular host."

"We can't ask Aaron to do that again."

"Even if you did, the spell likely wouldn't take him. No, it would need to be a new host."

"Okay. Then I'll do it."

"Except your protection spell won't allow it."

"Then lift it!"

"No."

She folded her arms and fixed me with a stern look. "I'm not going to hurt you, Amelia. Or allow you to hurt yourself."

"But that only leaves hurting someone else."

"Maybe. But that's your best option right now. Even if I lifted the protection spell, then what? You fall unconscious and what's the plan after that? Hope that Sarah and the others figure out the solution without me? Or hope that they listen to me when I fix it?"

I looked away, not wanting to admit that she was right, but not having an argument.

No one would listen to her if she figured out how to lift the spell, and I knew it.

And she was the best bet for figuring it out, because she was the one to develop the spell in the first place.

Which left me as the only bridge for that solution when she came up with it.

I sighed. "Even if I was going to concentrate the spell on someone else, I can't. The Slayers decided that you were to blame before I figured it out, and they figured that I must have been the student who helped you. Especially after Nature gave me her blessing. They've locked me in a cell with Energy draining wards."

"*Energy* draining, but your connection to Nature should still give you enough to do this. You're just guiding an existing spell, after all. The problem if you're trapped will be getting close to a target."

I bit my lip as I realised that that might not actually be a problem.

And that I might be able to take care of two birds with one stone.

"Michael said that he would be back tomorrow. He thinks that he can torture a way to break the spell out of me. If I concentrate it in him instead, it will solve the problem, and stop him from hurting me."

Maria frowned. "If you concentrate the spell in him, the rest of the Slayers will not take that lightly."

"Do you have another idea?"

Her silence was deafening.

I sighed. "Look, I don't want to hurt anyone. But if it has to be someone, the asshole that just threatened to torture me is probably the best bet."

Maria nodded. "Okay. Do you remember the spell well enough to guide it?"

"Yeah."

"Then good luck. And... I'm sorry. For causing all of this mess in the first place."

I shrugged. "If concentrating the curse in Michael works, then there's nothing to worry about."

"Other than Michael being cursed."

I suppressed a shudder at the reminder of the way Michael had manhandled me. And his threats of what he would do to me in the morning. "You know, I think I can live with that one."

I AWOKE WITH A GROAN.

I'd felt fine when visiting Maria, but back in the waking world, every cell ached with the absence of Energy.

Just how much had I come to rely on my magic since I'd broken through? How much had my body gotten used to it?

Beyond the aching, I felt hollow inside.

Almost numb.

I forced myself to sit up on the thinly carpeted floor, focusing on what Maria had told me.

My Energy may be gone, but I was still tied to Nature.

I looked around, but being inside, I didn't exactly have any plants to draw from.

I focused with the sight Nature had given me, but I couldn't see anything.

How was I supposed to do this?

Before I could answer that question, the door to the cell opened.

And Michael returned.

He smirked as he looked at me, and I wondered what he saw.

I felt clammy and shaky, and my stomach churned at the thought that Michael was looking at a pale, shaking girl.

Weak and defenceless.

Though the visage that I might be presenting upset me less than the thought that it was accurate.

If I couldn't figure out a way to draw from Nature, there was little I could do.

A wave of nausea washed over me at the thought.

I refused to be defenceless.

I couldn't be.

But Michael grabbed me by the arm, pulling me to my feet, and even the token resistance I tried to give refused to move my muscles.

"Now," he said, "ready to talk?"

I tried to tell him to go fuck himself, but even my throat wouldn't respond.

"Don't worry," he said, "pain will motivate you enough to reveal exactly where Maria is hiding. And then you can both burn for what you've done to this school. Proof that this experiment was always doomed to fail, and that Witches will always need the protection of Slayers."

I shivered as I realised that he'd likely never had any intention of finding a cure.

No, he had always been looking for a scapegoat.

The scary monster he could blame for everything.

He was going to pretend that a fucking sixteen-year-old girl was the enemy here.

And I wished that I could believe that it wouldn't work.

But no. I'd seen too many of Maria's memories to ever believe that.

Electricity crackled, once more wrapping around my limbs and stopping me from moving as Michael stepped back.

My skin burned where the electricity held me, but I had no way of getting loose.

Not without my connection to Nature.

Shit, how did Willow do it? Surely there weren't plants nearby every time she tried to connect to Nature.

No, her connection was to the air. She showed me how to draw life from plants, but her element was air.

Just as Lena's was water.

Except I didn't have an element. I wasn't an elemental being.

But I was tied to Nature, and the elements were her domain.

Maybe I wasn't tied to one element in particular, but that didn't mean that I didn't have any connection to them at all.

A wave of charge passed through the electricity binding me and I howled in pain, my muscles spasming as every nerve-ending in my body overloaded with screaming agony.

I tried to gasp for breath, but I was held too tight.

I realised that the sparks around Michael's hand were growing in intensity.

He was getting ready for another wave.

I turned to the air around me, focusing with Nature's sight.

This had to work.

If it didn't...

No, I couldn't let that thought take root.

This had to work.

As I focused on the air swirling around me, I started to see...

Well, it swirling.

The way it moved in and out of my and Michael's lungs, giving us strength.

But I needed more strength right now.

I needed as much as I could possibly get.

The air surged into my lungs, forcing its way in, despite my tight bindings.

And with it came strength.

The bindings around me snapped, letting me loose and dropping me to the ground.

"What the hell?"

I didn't give Michael an answer, simply reaching for my wand as strength, and Energy, flooded back into my system.

Thankfully, with the Energy draining wards, he hadn't thought to take my wand from me.

I grabbed it tight in my hand and turned to the life-force swirling around the school.

If it needed to take from someone, there was someone right here.

I fuelled my wand with my anger as I reformed Maria's spell, drawing the pattern I'd read in her grimoire in the air in front of me.

Michael tried to lunge forward, but his life force started to drain into the air around us, and he collapsed to his knees.

"You... What are you doing?" he managed to growl, but I ignored him.

"Amy?"

I turned at my auntie's voice to see her struggling to enter the room, leaning heavily on the door.

"Auntie Jess," I said as I rushed over to help her, forgetting the spell. "What's happening?"

"The spell that's draining everyone's life force. I think we and Aaron are the only ones left. I was staving it off with potions but... I guess I've run out of luck. I wanted to make sure you were okay, before..."

Her gaze drifted over to Michael. "The spell get him too?"

"I... I know how to end this. I just need to concentrate it on Michael and the rest of you will be safe, I promise. I just need to finish."

I went to turn back to Michael, but Auntie Jess stopped me with her hand on my arm.

"Wait, Amy... Concentrate it? You mean like when it was draining Aaron?"

"Yes. But we don't have another solution right now."

"But we weren't sure what damage that might have done if Aaron was left longer. Who knows if Michael will react the same way, or if this will hurt him more."

"Well, it has to be someone, and he was going to blame me for this entire incident. He never wanted a cure, he wanted this to end the school, and then he was going to string me up for it to give everyone a villain to hate."

Auntie Jess cringed. "I'm sorry, Amy. I should have realised. But if you do this, you can't go back. If this kills him..."

"I don't care. It's him or me." I knew that the words weren't true the second they were out of my mouth.

I *was* him or me.

But I did care.

Except caring was going to get me killed, so...

It was a luxury I couldn't afford.

I wouldn't let this bastard kill me and ride off into the sunset because I couldn't stomach the alternative.

That wasn't fair.

That wasn't just.

"You will care when you can never show your face in magical society ever again," Auntie Jess said. "He's trying to make you out to be the next Maria Brown by pinning this on you. If you concentrate it on him, that's what you'll become. You'll never be able to come back from that."

"I don't have a choice. There's no other way to wake everyone else up, and I can't concentrate it on myself."

"Then concentrate it on me."

I stared at her, my mind taking a moment to process her words. "What? No! I'm not going to-"

"You're right, you need to wake everyone up, and I'm the only one left awake to volunteer."

"No, I can't. What if it kills you?"

"Then it's not your fault. I'm taking on this risk, Amy. I'm volunteering. I know that you'll figure out how to wake me. And I also know that once Gail is awake, she'll know how to keep you safe from Michael. But if you concentrate the spell on him, the rest of the Slayers will have all of the ammunition they need to not only hunt you down, but also to close the school. I promised your parents that I would look after you, and I promised Gail that I would look after the school. I'm sick of breaking promises, Amy, don't make me break these two."

Tears welled in my eyes as I realised that she was right.

Maria had warned me as well – there would be consequences to concentrating the spell on Michael – but I had been so focused on the consequences for me, I hadn't thought about what would happen to the school.

But Auntie Jess was right, if Michael was cursed here, that would give the rest of the Slayers all of the ammunition they needed to shut the school down.

"Maybe it doesn't have to be you," I said. "Maybe I can break the protection spell keeping me safe-"

"No," Auntie Jess said firmly. "I won't allow it. Concentrate the spell on me, and don't blame yourself, Amy. I'm choosing this. I would rather it be me than you. Now do it, before I pass out. It might not work if the spell has already claimed me."

I bit my lip, knowing that she was right – I had to act fast – but the thought of hurting my auntie...

Auntie Jess slid down the doorframe a little and I realised that time was running out.

I gripped my wand and focused on the spell, redirecting it once more as I did my best to ignore the reality of what I was doing.

Of who I was concentrating the spell on...

Auntie Jess slid fully to the ground as the spell began to take form around her, ceasing its pull on anyone else as it settled into just drawing from a single source once more.

Her eyelids drooped, and I had to stop my hand from shaking as I realised that there were just moments left until the spell was complete.

"Amy," Auntie Jess managed, her voice terrifyingly weak, "Tell Gail... Tell her not to blame herself. That I was happy to fight for my home."

No, I couldn't do this. I couldn't...

But before I could finish that thought – before I could stop the spell – it was over.

The spell had a new host, and the rest of the school should awaken at any moment.

Silent tears flowed down my cheeks as I knelt beside my auntie.

Maybe it hadn't worked as well as last time. Maybe the spell was weak enough now that I could break it.

"*You!*" Michael spat before I could even consider trying to break the spell, scrambling to his feet. "You attacked me. I'll have your head for that."

"You were torturing me!"

Creator, why was he still trying to do this? Didn't he care that my auntie was hurt?

Didn't he realise that it was over?

Before either of us could say anything else, three more Slayers entered the room.

I tensed at first, but then spotted Chris – Sarah's husband – and wondered just how exactly this was going to go.

"Michael," Chris said as he entered. "We just woke up, and it looks like everyone else has too. Did you find a cure?" He then looked between the two of us and frowned. I'm sure neither of us looked pretty. Then his gaze fell on Auntie Jess and his frown deepened. "What happened here?"

"Grab that girl," Michael growled. "She's the one responsible for all of this, and when I tried to get the truth out of her, she attacked me. Then she attacked her aunt, putting her under the same spell that has been affecting everyone else."

"She told me to!" I quickly said, my voice more than a little pleading as I turned to Chris. "This curse that's been knocking people out, it was the binding spell Maria Brown placed on Mr Stiles. Sarah and I thought we'd dispelled it completely, but we just lifted it from him."

Chris sighed. "So, it started looking for other hosts?"

I nodded. "I don't know how to dispel it, but I did figure out how to concentrate it into one person again. My auntie told me to concentrate it on her." Tears welled in my eyes and I did everything I could to fight them back, but saying it aloud made it all too real. "I didn't want to, but she was the only one still awake except me and Michael, so she volunteered."

Chris folded his arms and turned to Michael. "And why didn't you volunteer? If you were awake as well, why did you allow a Witch to take on this sacrifice?"

"I... The girl is lying. She was the one to cast the binding spell in the first place!"

"No, Maria Brown was. And we'll soon be able to examine Jessica and see if it is, indeed, the same spell that affected one of the other members of staff. If it is, then I think that's all the proof we need that Amelia is telling the truth."

"But that girl worked with Maria Brown-"

"That girl passed the Amazon's trials."

"Which is why they refused to give us her name. But they cannot protect her now. Not after she did so much damage to the school."

"Damage that has now been reversed."

"Dana will not-"

"Dana is no longer in charge of the Amazons." Chris held up his phone. "Word came through just as we woke up. Esme has won the leadership competition. She trained Amelia personally during the trials. If you try to take her in, you risk starting a war."

Michael glared at him. "Then it's war. The Amazons are not so powerful that they can defy the Council of Light."

One of the Slayers beside Chris folded his arms. "No one will go to war on the orders of a Slayer who failed to protect those weaker than himself. Jessica should never have been given the chance to sacrifice herself for the school while you were in the room."

I was sure that Michael was going to pop a blood vessel at that, but he didn't argue.

So... was that it?

Was it truly over?

If Esme was in charge, could the Slayers truly not touch me now?

Chris turned to the others. "Come on. We should get Jessica to the infirmary." He turned to me. "Do you want me to shift you there, too? You look more than a little bruised."

"I... Yeah."

Michael turned to the others. "I will be filing a full report with the Council." He turned to me. "We might not be able to take on the Amazons alone, but the Council *will* hold them to account."

He narrowed his eyes, and I got the feeling that I knew exactly who he intended to hold to account.

I shivered at the thought before Chris placed his arm on my shoulder and shifted me out of there.

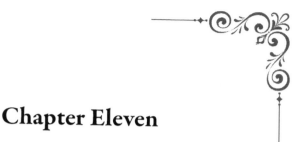

Chapter Eleven

We arrived to find the infirmary empty except for Sarah, Mr Stiles, and Ms Griffin.

"Sarah," Chris said as soon as he saw her, before rushing over and holding her tight.

She returned his embrace with equal force, burying her head in his neck. "I'm okay," she assured him. "We all woke up and are okay."

He eventually pulled away, and she smiled. "Everyone woke up, and we sent the students back to their rooms to recover. I was just about to go and find out what Michael had done with Amy..."

She turned to me at the same time as Ms Griffin spotted Auntie Jess being carried by one of the Slayers, out cold.

"What happened?" Ms Griffin asked as the Slayer lay Auntie Jess down on one of the beds.

I shifted awkwardly, unsure who she was asking, but then she turned her gaze to me and there was no doubt.

"I'm sorry," I said. "I tried to find another way, I really did. But... I realised that the spell knocking everyone out was the binding spell Maria Brown had used on Mr Stiles."

"I know, he told me."

"I didn't know how to lift it, but... I'd seen enough of Maria's notes to know how to concentrate it again. I couldn't use myself, and... Michael... He..."

Chris stepped forward. "I get the impression that Michael was behind those bruises covering Amelia's skin. And I also get the impression that they might have looked worse had she not had some healing."

I frowned. Healing? But then I remembered the surge of power I'd pulled from the air. "I went to Nature to ask for her help and she had me drink from a pool. When Michael had me captured, I realised that I could pull power from the air to break free. I guess that's what healed me..."

"Then what happened?"

"I... Well, I didn't even know if anyone else was even awake, and I knew that I didn't have time, and he had just tortured me, so..."

Gail sighed. "You tried to concentrate the spell on Michael?"

I looked away. "I didn't think that I had another option. But then Auntie Jess came. She was barely standing, but she said that if I used Michael, the Slayers would shut down the school and hunt me down. She offered herself up instead. I tried to find another way, I really did-"

Gail cut me off. "It's not your fault, Amelia. If anyone is to blame here, it's me. I should have realised what was happening sooner. I should have been the one to make the sacrifice. Hell, I should never have let Maria Brown fool me in the first place..."

"Auntie Jess told me to tell you not to blame yourself. She said that she was happy to do this to protect her home."

Gail let out a quiet, humourless snort as tears tracked down her cheeks and she took Auntie Jess' hand in hers. "You know," she said softly, and I got the impression that her words were for my auntie, not me, "when I said that I wanted you to think of this place as your home, this wasn't what I meant..."

Sarah then made her way over to me, examining me with her wand. "Well, nothing looks permanently damaged. I think you need rest and healing potions, just like everyone else. Though you might be the only one able to sleep right now..."

I just nodded.

"Did you hear about Esme?"

"That she won the leadership election? Yeah, Chris told Michael to stop him from keeping me with the Slayers."

"Keeping you with them?"

"Michael wanted to blame me and Maria for everything that had happened here. He figured that the incident would be enough to shut the school down, and then he would be praised as a hero for capturing Maria's accomplice."

Sarah sighed. "I want to say that that wouldn't have worked... That no one would fear a sixteen-year-old..."

"But I threaten their power. Yeah, I think I've grasped that one now."

"If you'd never met Maria, they might not be so scared. They might have thought that they could control and manipulate you. Though, given how quick you were to denounce the Amazons and their way of running things, maybe there was never hope of that."

"So, what? I should have just shut up when they were being clearly biased against my friends?"

"No. But you have made things harder for yourself by doing so. Michael isn't going to let this go, and he will likely find allies among the Amazons."

"Even after Esme has won?"

"Dana and her friends didn't disappear, Amelia. Esme won by a narrow margin, and there are already calls to know if all of the votes came from younger Amazons, with some starting to talk about possibly implementing a higher voting age in the future, given the prolonged lifespan of Witches."

"So, what? They're trying to take away our votes? But they can't, right? Not with Esme in charge?"

"Important issues still have to go to vote with the Amazon council, and you can bet that Dana and her friends will now start trying to tear things apart from the inside. They're already contesting my presence, saying that my previous ties to Freya make me a Demon plant."

"Wait, seriously?"

Sarah nodded. "We'll handle it, but this isn't over. Not with Michael on a mission."

My stomach twisted. "I've fucked this up for everyone, haven't I?"

"No, Amelia. What were you supposed to do? Let Michael kill you? No, Michael has had it out for this school from the beginning, and Esme was always going to defend it. You just ended up caught in the middle.

"Now, you should go and find your friends. I think you need the reminder that you actually saved everyone today."

I looked over to my auntie. "Not everyone..."

"No, but we'll figure out how to wake her up. I promise."

I nodded, not quite believing her, but making my way back to my room anyway.

AS I APPROACHED THE dormitories, I turned my attention back to my connection to Nature.

I wanted to see Willow, to make sure that she was okay, and I wondered if I could sense her through my new connection.

As soon as I started to look for her, I got my answer.

She shone through the sight, calling to me like a beacon.

I increased my pace, desperate to see her once more.

To speak to her in person, not to some fragment of her mind.

I was almost there before I realised that I was heading to my room.

Was she there, waiting for me?

As I rounded the corner just before my door, I found myself tackled into a tight hug, a blanket of crimson hair almost suffocating me.

But I didn't care as I returned the embrace with equal ferocity, my throat tightening at the feel of my girlfriend in my arms once more.

"You're okay," I breathed into her hair, having to say it to really believe it. "You're okay..."

"I am," Willow replied as she eventually pulled away. "And... I love you too, Amelia."

My heart jumped to my throat. "You... You remember?"

She nodded. "You sneaking into my thoughts? Yeah, I remember. I don't think I would have if you hadn't said... Well..."

"That I loved you?"

She nodded, her cheeks turning pink. "Yeah. That. But... Did you not think that I would? Did you not mean it?"

"I did mean it," I assured her hurriedly. "Willow, I... I meant it with everything I have, and when you were knocked out by the spell... I was so annoyed that I hadn't told you. I should have told you."

Willow surged forward, closing the space between us and kissing me with everything she had.

Raw Energy surged between us, but it wasn't like it had been in the past.

No, it was... *more.*

There was an intensity that pulled me in, like a tide pulling me under, and I didn't want it to let me go.

"Amelia," Willow managed as she finally pulled away, though she didn't go far. "Your magic... It feels..."

"I went to Nature for help."

Willow regarded me, her eyes widening after just a moment. "How did I not notice? Your eye..."

I smiled. "I think you were too busy kissing me."

At that, I closed the space between us once more, the Energy crackling between us.

Yes, I could feel it clearly now.

It was like... a lack of resistance.

Like being called home.

When Willow finally pulled away for air, she sighed. "I fucking hate that we have to have roommates..."

My cheeks heated as I smiled. "Want to take me back to your room?"

"Yes. But Maya has her friends in there right now. And while I waited out here to see you privately-"

"You waited in the corridor for privacy?"

"Charlotte, Natalie and Lena are all packed into your tiny room. Did you really want to talk in front of them all?"

"No, I guess not. Especially not when we're not just talking."

Willow sighed once more. "I'm sick of being sensible, Amelia. I'm sick of telling both you and myself that young magical beings are so emotional, so we can't rush into things. How many times have I almost watched you die since we met? And now..."

"And now you were the one hurt?"

She nodded. "I'd never forgive myself if something happened to either of us and we'd been holding back." She then stepped back, looking to the door of my room. "But the others are worried about you. And there's nowhere we could go for privacy anyway, so..."

I leaned forward and kissed her gently, doing everything I could not to get lost in the feel of her once more.

She was right, we had other things to focus on.

"I don't want to hold back anymore either," I told her. "And I really am sorry for scaring you in the past. After watching that spell take you... I don't think I could do that again."

She gave me a small smile. "Then I'll try to stay out of trouble."

I smiled back. "Why do I get the feeling that that's not a promise either of us can keep?"

"Because you're very astute."

I shook my head before taking her hand and turning back to the door to my room.

I opened the door to see that Natalie, Lena and Charlotte were, indeed, waiting for us, with Lena and Charlotte sitting on Natalie's bed, while Natalie sat on mine.

"Lia!" Lena said with a smile as I entered. "So, what happened? You weren't in the infirmary when we woke up. Were you one of the last ones to go?"

I shook my head. "No, Maria cast a protection spell on me, and it stopped the binding spell from draining my life force."

Lena frowned. "Binding spell? That's what it was?"

I cringed as I sat down on the edge of my bed, Willow going to sit next to me. "It was the binding spell Maria cast on Mr Stiles."

"Shit. A Maria Brown spell... We were lucky to wake up at all..."

At that, Charlotte leaned further into her, and I frowned as I realised that she was practically draped over her.

Like a cat that wasn't getting enough attention.

Lena raised an eyebrow as she turned to her. "Are you okay? You've been super touch-y since you woke up."

Charlotte frowned, pulling away. "I... You don't usually mind that."

"I'm not saying that I *mind* it. I'm just saying that... It's not usual for you. You usually only get that close when you're upset about something."

Charlotte groaned, shaking her head as she backed further away from Lena, pulling her knees tight to her chest. "Why am I so bad at this? It's the house on Themiscyra all over again. I don't know the words, so I can't put them in place, and then it's all just..."

Lena cringed. "Yeah, I actually... I meant to talk to you about that. I promised I would when you woke up. I'm sorry. It was really thoughtful of you to get a house by the beach for me, and I... I was scared of reading too much into it, so I teased you, rather than just talking about it, even though I know you hate that."

Charlotte still didn't meet her gaze, mumbling her next words into her knees so that I almost missed them. "You wouldn't have been reading anything into it. That's what I was trying to say, but doing a really bad job of... I'm not good with words, Lena, so I just... I thought

I would show you with the house, but then that didn't go as planned and..."

I frowned, pretty sure that this wasn't a conversation they should be having in front of the rest of us.

Though, it also looked like a conversation that wasn't actually going to go anywhere without any help...

"Just tell her you love her," Willow, Natalie and I blurted out at the same time.

Lena and Charlotte just turned and stared at the three of us.

Charlotte, surprisingly, was the first to find her words. "Which... Which one of us?"

I sighed, giving her a sympathetic look. "Either. Both. I don't care, but this is getting painful."

Lena then turned to Charlotte. "Is she... Are they right about...?"

Charlotte nodded. "I'm sorry, I know that it makes things awkward. Just because you like girls doesn't mean that you like me, and it took me so long to even figure out what I was feeling, that even if you had once liked me, I would understand if you got tired of waiting-"

Lena was on her faster than I could track, hungrily capturing Charlotte's lips with hers.

Charlotte stiffened, and then melted into her, and Willow, Natalie and I all looked away.

"Should we... You know... Remind them we're here?" Willow whispered after an uncomfortable few moments, when it became clear that Charlotte and Lena were showing no signs of slowing down.

I grimaced. "I feel bad stopping them when this has clearly been simmering away for a while."

Natalie sighed. "They do have their own room. They could return there."

I nodded, figuring that she was right as I cleared my throat as loud as I could.

I needed to keep clearing my throat for several moments, but the two of them finally pulled away from each other.

"Right," Lena said, a little breathless. "We're not alone..."

Charlotte turned bright red, as if she'd just remembered that fact herself.

I gave them both a sympathetic smile. "It's understandable. Just... awkward for the rest of us."

Lena nodded with a smile as she cuddled up next to Charlotte once more, in a thankfully platonic way. "Yeah, sorry. Okay, different topic. So, Lia, how did you save the day?"

I looked away, the amusement of my friends getting together quickly doused by the memory of that morning.

Of what I'd had to do to wake them.

It took me several moments to find my words again. "I... I didn't have time to untangle Maria's binding spell entirely. So, my auntie told me to concentrate it again, using her as the host."

Lena and Charlotte suddenly looked a lot less happy as Willow placed a hand on my shoulder. "I'm sorry, Amelia."

"It's okay. We'll figure out how to dispel it for good." I managed to speak with far more confidence than I felt, and Willow's gentle squeeze on my shoulder told me that she knew, but she didn't say anything.

"Yeah," Lena said. "You managed to wake the rest of us up, so one more person can't be too hard, right?"

I tried to ignore the argumentative voice in my head, telling me that Lena was wrong.

That I couldn't do this...

But then Willow leaned in closer to me, and I couldn't help but melt into her, the feel of her magic drawing me in like a warm blanket.

It was just so... *her*, and I didn't want to be anywhere else.

"How about we talk about something else," Willow said, and I gave her a small smile of gratitude.

Though as I took Willow's hand in mine, my thumb gently stroking the back of hers, I spotted Natalie sitting silently at the end of the bed, her Vampire nature probably making her impossible to read to most.

But I couldn't help but notice the slight tightness in her frame, and the dull sadness behind her eyes.

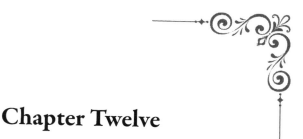

Chapter Twelve

Maria smiled as I arrived back in her lab that night.
"Amelia! Are you okay?"

I nodded. "Yeah, I am."

"And you managed to concentrate the spell on the Slayer?"

I cringed, looking away. "My auntie caught me before I could and insisted that I use her so as not to antagonise the Slayers. But the way Michael was talking... I don't think he's going to leave this alone. He's determined to take both of us down, even if everyone but my auntie recovering means that he can't really pin the curse on us. I mean, he can, but people won't be out for blood as much."

Maria sighed. "It sounds like you wounded his pride. That will make him more dangerous."

I bit my lip, less than happy at the thought.

Maria gave me a reassuring smile. "But let's leave that for another day. We'll wait for him to make the first move, and we'll go from there. For now, we'll focus on saving your aunt and cleaning up this mess once and for all."

"Do you really think that we can do it?"

"Actually, I spent all day going over my old notes, and I think I have a promising lead..."

I AWOKE WITH A PAIR of soft arms wrapped around me, and I snuggled into Willow instinctively as I remembered that we'd just drifted off while talking with the others.

But as much as I wanted nothing more than to stay snuggled against her, my ADHD quickly set in, leaving me restless, and I turned over to find my phone.

I sighed as I realised that it was three in the morning...

Why was I up?

But then, I supposed that after the stress of the last few days, insomnia was the least I could expect.

I turned over to see Charlotte and Lena curled up, fast asleep in blankets on the floor.

But Natalie's bed was empty.

I frowned as I looked around the room, grabbing my wand and casting a night vision spell.

But no, Natalie wasn't there.

And the bathroom light wasn't on, so I assumed she wasn't in there either.

But then I spotted that the window was open.

I turned to the new sense Nature had awakened in me, wondering if I could sense Natalie, even though she wasn't connected to Nature.

When I first opened the sense, I was quickly enveloped by the feel of Willow, like a warm breeze wrapping around me.

I wanted nothing more than to melt into the feeling and go back to sleep, but I couldn't deny that I was a little concerned about Natalie's absence.

So, I pushed my sense out across the room, and quickly shivered as I felt a biting, salty taste.

Like standing by the North Sea in the middle of winter, the water angry and tumultuous.

Lena.

Next to her, I sensed a flow of Energy, steady and calm.

Charlotte. I couldn't sense her as strongly as the other two, but she was still there, calming Lena's tides.

I stretched out, sensing weaker presences, like Charlotte.

But then I stretched out the sense above, and I was suddenly struck by what felt like a box of angry bees, banging up against thick, soundproof walls.

Thick walls that were starting to crack.

Natalie.

So, she was upset.

I suppressed a sigh before pulling myself from Willow's arms.

The air felt cold without her, and I was sorely tempted to just lie back down next to her.

But no, no one else was awake to talk to Natalie, and I didn't want to let her stew alone in whatever was upsetting her.

I focused on where I could sense her, before closing my eyes, and attempting to shift up next to her.

I stumbled as the ground fell out from beneath me.

"Hey, careful!"

Strong arms grabbed me, keeping me steady as I opened my eyes to see that I was on the roof.

With Natalie standing next to me, holding me tight.

"Thanks," I said.

"It's okay," she said as she carefully pulled away, allowing me to find my footing as she sat down once more.

I sat down next to her, careful not to fall off the edge.

"Are you all right?" I asked once I was sitting safely. "It's the middle of the night."

"I couldn't sleep. But I'm okay, really. Just... The binding spell kept me asleep for ages, and my natural cycle is nocturnal. It's probably going to take a while to get it back to normal."

"Okay," I said.

"But I really am okay. You don't have to stay here with me. You should go back to bed."

I shrugged. "I don't think that I could if I tried. My insomnia gets worse with stress, and I think I've been more than a little stressed lately."

"Yeah, I can imagine..."

I waited several moments before sighing, knowing that I couldn't just leave it alone. "Are you sure that you're okay? When Lena said that the binding spell had shown her what really mattered... Well, you didn't look happy."

Natalie sighed. "I just... It wasn't so bad before. Before Lena and Charlotte finally stopped ignoring the obvious. But now they're together and you're with Willow, and I just... I'm tired, Amy. I'm tired of the rules constraining me. I'm sick of watching my friends find love when I'm not allowed. Of finding people that I care about and having to back away, not because either of us don't like each other, but because it's too dangerous."

"I'm sorry," I said, not sure what else I could say, more than aware that I was one of the people that she'd had to back away from. "If seeing me with someone else bothers you..."

"No, Amy, it's not... I would never want you to not be with Willow. You deserve to have someone who can be with you. I just... I understand the risks. I'm not saying I'm going to do anything reckless. I just... I wish that the risks weren't there, you know?" She sighed. "Do you ever wish that you were just normal?"

I shrugged. "I'm not sure what 'normal' would even mean. I mean, 'normal' for me has always meant neurotypical, and that... That's scary. Do I wish that I wasn't so forgetful, or that doing basic things was easier for me? Sure. But changing that would mean changing how my brain works. I'm fine topping up my focus with medication, but changing my brain permanently? No. I wouldn't be me anymore if I did. So, I guess I've just learned to take the bad with the good."

Natalie sighed. "Yeah, I know what you mean. I don't want to be different. A version of me that was just a Witch or just a Vampire wouldn't be *me*. But... I do wish things were simpler."

"Yeah," I agreed. "Simpler would be nice..."

Dear Reader

So, we've reached the half-way point of the series!

It's so weird to have a series go so fast, most of my others have had longer between the first few books, but it's super exciting for everyone to be able to see what I've got planned.

Honestly, it's so hard not to spoil everything – there were several beta comments that had me almost cackling about what I knew was coming – so I will just leave you for now.

Special Thanks

I just wanted to give a shout out to my Patreon supporters as well as everyone who has left reviews of my books!

My Patreon supporters are a massive help to me being able to do this as my job (or, well, one of them... Cue a joke about being a millennial in this economy while I cry over my two degrees...) and reviews are a massive help to me being able to do this emotionally. Seriously, they make my day and everyone who has left one deserves cookies!

Want to Keep in Touch?

If you want to connect with me and other fans of the series between books, I have a weekly newsletter where we discuss things like the best fantasy soundtracks to work to and which vampire lore is the best, and there's also a closed Facebook group where I talk about secret projects that aren't ready to be shown anywhere else just yet.

You can find all of these places at lcmawson.com/links

Other Series by L.C. Mawson

Snowverse
Ember Academy for Young Witches
lcmawson.com/emberacademy
Ember Academy for Magical Beings
lcmawson.com/ember-academy-for-magical-beings
Freya Snow – YA/NA Urban Fantasy
lcmawson.com/books/freyasnow
The Royal Cleaner – F/F Urban Fantasy
lcmawson.com/books/the-royal-cleaner
Engineered Rebel – Sci-fi/Urban Fantasy
lcmawson.com/engineered-rebel
Castaway Heart – Mermaid Romance (CW for Steamy Scenes and Domestic Violence)
lcmawson.com/castawayheart
Other
Aspects – YA Sci-fi
lcmawson.com/the-aspects
The Lady Ruth Constance Chapelstone Chronicles – Steampunk Novellas
lcmawson.com/books/ladyruth

Printed in Great Britain
by Amazon